ADVENTURE ON WHALEBONE ISLAND

M. A. Wilson

Illustrations by Vadym Prokhorenko

Rainy Bay Press
Gibsons, BC

Published by Rainy Bay Press
PO Box 1911
Gibsons, BC
V0N 1V0

www.rainybaypress.ca

ISBN: 978-0-9953445-0-1

For Lucy

Table of Contents

~ 1 ~

Summer Holidays

Ryan and Kendra stood on the lower deck of the ferry as the massive steel doors swung slowly open, the foamy sea swirling in front of them as the ship approached the terminal. The ferry shuddered and swayed as it docked, and both children held tightly to their suitcases to keep their balance. At the top of the ramp a large number of people were waiting. They strained to see their aunt in the crowd. Suddenly a woman in a large floppy sunhat pushed her way to the front and began waving madly. Ryan and Kendra looked at each other and grinned as they waved back. At that moment the gate lifted and they followed the other passengers up the ramp, their suitcases bumping roughly on the metal walkway.

"Kendra! Ryan! How wonderful to see you," exclaimed Aunt Jennie, throwing her arms around them. "My, look how you've grown!"

Ryan rolled his eyes. "I haven't grown at all in the last year," he said glumly.

"That's true," said Kendra. "He's the shortest one in his class now. Even Billy is taller than him, and Billy's nickname is Shorty!"

"Not to worry," said his aunt. "We'll just have to

stuff you full of yummy food to make you grow faster. Here, have this," and she pulled a cheese scone out of the cloth bag she was carrying. Taking Kendra by the hand, she led them up the walkway.

Ryan followed behind, pulling his suitcase and munching on his cheese scone. That was one thing he remembered about Aunt Jennie, she was a fabulous cook. His own parents were rarely home from work early enough to cook a real meal and most of their dinners seemed to come out of the microwave. He took another bite of the scone. It was light and flaky and delicious, not at all like the dry crumbly things his mother occasionally brought home from the office.

It was two years since Ryan and Kendra had last seen Aunt Jennie and Uncle William and their cousins Claire and Nathan. Back then they had only come to the house in Rainy Bay for a weekend, as their parents had to be back at work on Monday. But for two glorious days they had played on the beach, swam in the ocean, collected shells and little crabs, and eaten Aunt Jennie's enormous home-cooked meals. When it was time to leave, Kendra had hidden under a boat on the beach and refused to come out, and they nearly missed the ferry.

Now they were back for almost two weeks while their parents were in Europe for a conference. Although Ryan was excited about the prospect, he was also a little nervous. What if Claire and Nathan didn't want to play with them? He wasn't too concerned about Nathan, who was younger, but Claire was a year older than him and two years older than Kendra. Now that two years had passed, she was probably more interested in her own friends. Uncle William also worried him a little. He always seemed to be walking around half naked and cursing like a pirate, picking them up and throwing them off the end of the dock whenever he got the chance. But what worried Ryan the most, although he didn't want to admit it to himself, was that perhaps this visit might not live up to his memories of the last one.

* * *

Aunt Jennie led them to a small blue car in the parking lot. They put their suitcases in the trunk and climbed into the back seat. As Aunt Jennie drove along the winding road, glimpses of the sea could be seen through the trees. It was a sunny day and the water sparkled. Here and there boats were moored off the shore, and the roofs of cottages poked up at the end of long driveways. After driving a few kilometres they came to the village of Maple Harbour.

"Lots of development going on these days," said Aunt Jennie. "I hardly recognize the place." Ryan and Kendra looked at each other. The village wasn't very big and seemed like it hadn't changed much in decades. Nothing looked newly constructed.

"Oh, I know," laughed their aunt, glancing at their expressions in the car's rearview mirror. "It probably doesn't look much different to you. But there's been a number of new houses this year and down the road a bit they're building a new marina and hotel. That's a lot of change for around here."

Kendra recalled that her aunt was a member of the local town council, so she always knew the details of what was going on in Maple Harbour.

The road continued to wind along the seashore for a few kilometres. Shortly, Aunt Jennie turned off onto a dirt road. It was bumpy and rutted and their aunt had to drive slowly to avoid bottoming out the small car. They were in thick forest now, with tall cedar and fir trees towering over them. They reached a clearing where a number of other vehicles were parked. Aunt Jennie pulled in next to a battered old pickup truck and switched the engine off.

The children got out of the car and followed their aunt down a dirt trail until they came out of the forest. Ahead of them stood an old cottage with white clapboard siding and a moss covered roof. At the front was a bright red door. Each window had a red trim and a blue flower box beneath it. To Ryan and Kendra, whose home was much more modern and suburban, it seemed like something from a fairy tale. On one side an extension had been built, in the same clapboard style, where Ryan recalled his cousins having their bedrooms.

As they stood a dog came racing out of the garden and skidded to a stop in front of them. It immediately went up to Ryan and pushed its nose against his leg, gazing up with big pleading eyes. Ryan kneeled down and began to pet the dog, who promptly lay down at his feet and rolled over on its back.

"Oh Meg," sighed Aunt Jennie.

Kendra bent over to give Meg a pet. "You've got a new dog?"

"Yes, we picked her up from the SPCA a few months ago. She's a very sweet dog, but she'd like you to pet her all day long." Hearing her name, Meg wagged her tail. "She's part Labrador retriever and that's the problem. Labs live on ten percent food and ninety percent love." Aunt Jennie gave her a quick pat on the head and then shooed her away.

A winding stone path led through a garden filled with shrubs and flowers. Ryan and Kendra followed their aunt along this path to the front door. Aunt Jennie pushed it open and stepped into the house. Inside it seemed cool and dark after the bright sunshine outside. The children blinked and looked around. At the front was a bright red door. Each window had red trim and a blue flower box beneath it.

The walls of the hallway were covered in strange artifacts from around the world. Masks from Africa, clay pots from Central America, antique weapons and musical instruments from Asia, as well as paintings, carvings, and all kinds of other curios. Uncle William had travelled the world when he was young and worked in a number of different countries. Along the way he had collected most of these items, although a few had been contributed by Aunt Jennie, who also loved to travel.

"I'm not sure where Claire and Nathan are," Aunt Jennie said as she ushered them down the hallway. "Probably at the beach. I'll show you to your rooms so you can put your suitcases away. Then you can go look for them."

"What about Uncle William?" asked Kendra, who found her uncle fascinating and never tired of listening to his stories.

"Oh, he's out and about," replied her aunt with a laugh. "I'm never quite sure where, but he'll be back for lunch. Now here's Claire's room, where you'll be sleeping Kendra."

She opened the door to Claire's bedroom. Everything was tidy and the bed was carefully made up. Pictures of boats lined the walls, including a large poster of a sailboat with waves crashing over its bow. Along the window ledge were a number of small trophies with sailboats on them. Kendra walked over to examine them. They all had Claire's name on them.

Aunt Jennie had already moved down the hall to another room. This was Nathan's and was the opposite of Claire's in terms of order and cleanliness. Aunt Jennie sighed as she looked in. The floor was covered in clothes and books, with a large half-finished jigsaw puzzle in the middle. There was a double bunk bed on one side of the room and the bottom bunk was covered in more clothes and books. The top bunk was clear but had not been made.

"He promised me that he had got the room ready for you," Aunt Jennie said with a touch of exasperation.

"Oh that's all right," said Ryan, heaving his suitcase onto the top bunk. He was secretly relieved. He knew Kendra would have a hard time keeping Claire's room that neat; her own room back home looked more like Nathan's most of the time.

Once they had settled into their rooms, Ryan and Kendra made their way back to the kitchen where Aunt Jennie was busy preparing lunch. "Why don't you two go down to the dock and look for Claire and Nathan?" she suggested. "They're sure to be down there somewhere. You can tell them lunch will be ready shortly."

Ryan and Kendra made their way across the lawn

that sloped down in front of the house. At the bottom of the lawn was a thick hedge and beyond that a steep embankment. In the middle of the hedge was a wooden gate, which the children pushed open and stepped through. They both paused and gazed at the view.

In front of them lay a picture perfect bay with greeny-blue water that sparkled in the sunlight. In the middle of the bay was a small sandy beach which sloped gently down to the water. Above the high tide line it was piled high with driftwood. The remainder of the shoreline was rocky and steep, and above the rocks were arbutus trees, strange twisting trees with thin peeling bark that left their reddish orange branches exposed. A rickety set of steps tumbled down the hillside to a small boathouse and a sturdy looking dock. At the end of the dock, a small boy sat facing the sea, reading a book. In front of him, a small sailboat sped across the mouth of the bay, its sails full and a blue flag fluttering at the masthead.

It looks like a scene from a postcard, thought Ryan. But his thoughts were interrupted by an angry yell from below. "Go away! Go away!"

In front of them lay a picture perfect bay.

2

Sunken Treasure

Ryan and Kendra both jumped, thinking the words were directed at them. The boy had jumped to his feet and was swinging his arms wildly, with an angry scowl on his face. Kendra and Ryan hesitated, wondering what to do.

Suddenly the boy stopped shouting, looked up at them, and gave a friendly wave. Nervously the two of them made their way down the stairs to the dock, with Meg following behind. Out in the bay, the little sailboat had turned and was now returning toward shore. At the end of the dock stood their cousin Nathan.

"Sorry about that," he said, pushing his hair back out of his eyes. "There was a wasp buzzing around while I was trying to read! There's a nest in the trees at the other end of the beach, but they don't usually bother us down here." Nathan was a tall gangly boy with long shaggy hair that fell over his eyes. He was the same height as Ryan, although he was two years younger.

Kendra and Ryan looked at each other, relieved to know the yelling had been directed at a wasp and not at them.

"I'm really glad you've come," he continued. "It's

going to be a great summer with all of us here!" He looked out to sea, where the little sailboat was now quite close. In it was a girl with long sandy coloured hair, watching the sail intently. She glanced toward the dock and gave them a quick wave.

Claire guided the sailboat straight toward the dock. "Look out!" she called and Ryan and Kendra hurriedly backed away from the edge of the dock. Nathan was already standing a safe distance back. Just as Ryan was sure she was about to crash into the dock, Claire pushed the tiller hard to one side and the little boat spun around quickly into the wind, parallel to the dock. At the same time she let go of the rope in her hand and the sail swung across the dock and stopped, flapping in the wind. Claire stepped out neatly and quickly wrapped a rope around a cleat on the edge of the dock. She stood up and faced the others.

"Welcome to Pirate Cove!" she said with a smile.

"I thought it was called Rainy Bay?" said Ryan, looking confused.

Claire looked at him doubtfully. "Well, that might be what it says on the map, but we think Pirate Cove is a much better name," she said. "Besides, it never rains here!" She laughed. Everyone knows there is always plenty of rain on the BC coast!

"Is this your boat?" asked Kendra.

"Yes," answered Claire. "This is *Pegasus*. I got her

two years ago, just after you were here."

"So that's why you have that flag," said Ryan, looking up at the little blue flag fluttering in the breeze. It was light blue with a black border. In the middle was a leaping black horse with wings. Pegasus, the flying stallion of ancient Greek mythology. "I thought Pegasus was white?" he said.

Claire shrugged. "Black shows up better. Anyway, *Pegasus* flies like the wind and is the fastest boat around. I'm going to teach you all to sail this summer and then we can go anywhere we like. There are all sorts of islands and coves to explore. And," she said, lowering her voice, "we're going to search for sunken treasure!"

"Oooh, really?" said Kendra. "I'd love to find a sunken wreck! When can we start?"

"There can't be any treasure," said Ryan. "There were never any treasure ships in this part of the world. And if there were they'd have been discovered ages ago."

"Well, maybe not exactly treasure," said Claire. "But there are sunken ships."

"That's right!" said Nathan. "Dad says there's a sunken wreck that's never been found not too far from us. Ask him about it at lunch."

"Speaking of lunch, I'm starving!" said Claire. The others agreed and together they set off up the stairs.

* * *

Back at the house, Aunt Jennie had prepared a large plate of sandwiches, with thick slices of bread cut from a freshly baked loaf. The children ate them quickly and then began munching on blueberries picked from the garden. As they were finishing, a vehicle arrived and a few moments later the front door swung open. Uncle William strode in wearing Bermuda shorts smudged with oil and an old grubby t-shirt with holes in it.

"Aha! You made it, I see." He picked Kendra up and swung her around and then held out his hand to Ryan, after wiping it quickly on his shorts.

"My, look how you've grown," he said. Ryan grimaced and Kendra giggled. "I'm glad you two could come for the summer. You'll have much more fun here than tramping around Europe!"

"It's going to be great!" said Nathan. "Finally I have someone besides Claire to play with. All she does is sail around in *Pegasus* all day."

"We're all going to be sailing around in *Pegasus* this summer," said Kendra. "Claire has promised to teach us how to sail. And then we're going to look for sunken wrecks and treasure!"

"Can you both swim?" asked Uncle William, looking at Kendra dubiously.

"Yes," said Ryan. "Kendra's quite good," he added.

"Yes, your mother told me that you're quite the swimmer," said Aunt Jennie. "Top swimmer in your age group, isn't it?" Kendra nodded shyly.

"What's this treasure all about?" Ryan asked his uncle. "There weren't any galleons or pirates around here."

"That's not true," said his uncle. "There's some evidence that Sir Francis Drake, the Elizabethan privateer, may have been the first European to sail around these parts. And the Spanish were certainly here.

"But I didn't say there was a treasure," he continued. "I just said there was a sunken wreck. A few years ago a motor boat called the *Gypsy Moth* was stolen from a house up the coast. It was a beautiful old wooden boat, a real classic. I remember seeing it a few times at the marina and it always had a crowd of people standing around looking at it.

"The night it was stolen a big storm blew up and a number of boats were damaged. The next morning a life ring was found on a beach near here with the name *Gypsy Moth* on it. The police did some investigation and a search was launched, but the boat was never found."

"How do they know it was stolen?" asked Ryan. "And didn't just blow away in the storm?"

"It was locked inside a boathouse and the lock was cut off," answered his uncle. "Boats don't get stolen very often around here. They're too hard to hide or to sell. If they do get stolen it's usually just joyriders who take them for the thrill and then leave them on a beach somewhere. Since the *Gypsy Moth* never turned up, people assume it must have sunk in the storm."

"Who would have stolen it?" asked Kendra.

"There are a few unsavoury characters around here that have been known to steal boats for fun. Ever since that night I've heard rumours it was a local fellow who stole it. People think he hit an unexpected rock during the storm. I'm pretty sure the boat is out there somewhere, although it may be in water too deep to access. As far as treasure goes, you won't find any gold, but who knows what you might find on board? At the very least, I'm sure the owner and the police would be very grateful if you could locate it."

"But how can we find it if a police search didn't turn anything up?" asked Ryan skeptically.

"That's what I thought," said Claire. "But dad said the police search wasn't very thorough. They were short-staffed at the time and weren't interested in putting a lot of time into searching for a boat that hadn't even made a distress call."

"And no people were reported missing so Search and Rescue didn't get involved," added Uncle William.

"It sounds exciting," said Kendra enthusiastically. "When can we start?"

3

Sailing Lessons

After lunch the four children changed into their swimsuits and went back down to the beach, carrying towels around their necks.

"Who's ready for some sailing lessons?" asked Claire.

"I am!" said Kendra eagerly. She glanced at Ryan, who was looking rather dubiously at the small boat bobbing up and down beside the dock. Ryan tended to avoid any sort of sporting activity. When he was younger his parents had enrolled him in an endless succession of activities – soccer, baseball, football, tennis, and numerous others. After each game he would return home humiliated by his lack of athletic ability. Football had been the worst; he had been knocked flat by a much larger boy on his very first play. That was the last straw and from then on Ryan had refused to participate in any more sports. He preferred puzzles and problem solving. He liked to take things apart and put them back together and was always being called upon to fix his friends' toys or his parents' computers. Ryan wasn't sure if sailing really qualified as a sport but he was pretty sure it was something he wouldn't like. However, he wasn't going to start off the summer holidays by refusing to go sailing.

"I guess so," he said after a bit.

"Good. Here are your lifejackets," said Claire. "Make sure they're done up tightly. Even if you are a good swimmer, you don't want to be overboard without one of these." Ryan and Kendra put them on and did them up.

Claire directed them into the boat and told them where to sit. Untying the bow line, she pushed the boat away from the dock and stepped lightly aboard. She took hold of the tiller and steered them out to sea. The light breeze filled the sail and *Pegasus* glided forward, small waves lapping at the bow.

"Okay," said Claire. "The first rule of sailing is to keep your head down." She looked at their blank faces and laughed. She pointed at the big metal pole that ran along the bottom of the sail. "That's the boom," she said. "And that's the sound it will make if it hits you on the head. Whenever we turn, which is called tacking, that boom will swing from one side of the boat to the other. You need to make sure your head is down when it does. So if I yell 'Going about!' or 'Tack!' it means we're about to turn and you should duck your heads.

"The other thing to remember is that we have to keep the boat balanced. That means we can't all be on one side at the same time. Unless the wind is really strong and we need all the weight on one side to counteract it. But on a day like today we need to spread out on both sides."

Ryan and Kendra nodded dumbly, sitting frozen in their places with their heads bent over.

"You don't need to hunch over like that; the boom isn't that low!" laughed Claire. "Just be aware of where it is and remember to duck when we tack. Besides, everyone gets hit by the boom at least once; it's the best reminder to keep your head down."

They straightened up a bit and began to relax as Claire went over the different ropes and parts of the boat, explaining what they were for. She told them how to set the sail according to what direction the wind was coming from and explained how it was possible to sail upwind by sailing back and forth at an angle. She demonstrated some basic knots and how to wrap the ropes around the cleats on the side of the boat. Lastly, she showed them how to steer the boat and set the sail by watching the little telltale ribbons on the sail.

"Of course, you have to watch where you're going as well. It's easy to spend too much time watching the ribbons and forget where you're going," she said.

After a while she asked Ryan to take over the tiller. He nervously agreed and shuffled to the back of the boat, keeping an eye on the boom as he went.

"Keep going in this direction," ordered Claire. "But you can move the tiller around a bit to get a sense of how the boat responds. Just don't make any big shifts."

Ryan held the tiller tightly and kept his eyes glued to the sail. It filled with wind and *Pegasus* moved ahead steadily. After a while he relaxed somewhat and began to experiment with turning the tiller one way and then the other, watching the little boat adjust to the new direction. Claire watched him and adjusted the sail as he made changes.

"Let's tack and go in that direction," she said, pointing to the opposite shore of the bay. Ryan nodded and called out "Ready... going about!" as Claire had instructed them. He pushed the tiller hard over and *Pegasus* came about, the boom swinging over their heads. Ryan quickly settled the boat into the new direction as Claire pulled in the main sheet. Surprisingly, it seemed to go exactly as he intended. Ryan was good at math and physics and everything Claire had explained had made perfect sense to him. But he was pleased to find that it worked in practice as well. Perhaps sailing was more like a puzzle than a sport. At least no one is going to knock me over, he thought.

Kendra watched Ryan carefully and was happy to see him smiling. She knew how much Ryan detested sports and how frustrated he could get when he wasn't good at something. This was sometimes made harder by the fact that Kendra excelled in almost every activity. But Ryan seemed to have taken to sailing like a duck to water.

After a while it was Kendra's turn at the tiller. She jumped at the opportunity, anxious to try her hand at steering. But she found it more difficult than she had anticipated. The boat never seemed to go in a straight line, and often the sail flapped as she brought it too close to the wind. She tried to watch the ribbons on the sail but kept mixing them up, so after a while she just aimed for a point on the shore and tried to keep in that direction.

She managed to complete a tack, although not as neatly as Ryan had done, and picked a new point on the opposite shore at which to aim. Suddenly there was a splash on the opposite side of the boat.

"Look, a seal!" cried Ryan. "There he is again! He's looking at us!"

Kendra leaned over to look in the direction Ryan was pointing. As she did so she took her eyes off the shore and *Pegasus* slowly turned into the wind.

"Watch where you're going!" cried Claire. Kendra looked ahead and quickly pushed the tiller over to correct the direction they were going. But in her haste she got confused and turned the wrong way. Suddenly *Pegasus* lurched over and the boom swung across, catching Kendra on the shoulder. As the wind was light the blow from the boom did not hurt, but it knocked her off balance. She dropped the tiller and fell backwards.

The next thing she knew there was a shock of cold water as she landed in the sea.

Spluttering and wiping the water from her eyes, she could see *Pegasus* about 15 feet away, its sail flapping in the wind. Claire was grinning and hooting loudly. Ryan looked shocked, but once he saw that Kendra wasn't hurt he began to laugh too. She swam back to the boat and pulled herself in with the help of the others.

"You can't say I didn't warn you!" laughed Claire. Kendra was laughing now as she sat on the side, dripping water into the boat. Once she got over the shock, she had found the dunking to be quite refreshing. But she shook her head when Claire asked if she wanted to take over the tiller again.

"Well, watching you in the water has made me think it's time for a swim," said Claire. "Shall we go back?"

The others nodded in agreement so Claire turned *Pegasus* around and headed back to shore. As they approached, a large fishing boat came around the point at high speed. It was heading directly toward them. Ryan glanced at Claire, but she seemed unconcerned.

"They'll move away," she said, noticing Ryan's look. "Sailboats have the right of way over motor boats." But the fishing boat continued to head straight for them. It was pushing a large bow wave in front of it. As it got closer Claire started to look more worried.

"What do they think they're doing?" she muttered.

"They can't possibly not see us!" She turned the tiller slightly to get out of the way of the other boat. But the boat changed course as well, continuing to aim toward them. It was now less than 20 metres away, and closing the gap quickly!

The boat was heading straight for them.

4

A Plan

"Hang on!" said Claire and she pushed the tiller over hard. *Pegasus* turned sharply toward the shore just as the fishing boat roared past, sounding its horn with a noisy blast. In the cabin they could see a thin man with a ponytail leering at them through the window and laughing. Claire shook her fist at him briefly but quickly had to turn her attention back to steering *Pegasus*. The wake from the fishing boat lifted them up and they shot toward the shore. Claire turned sharply again and as she did the wave tipped the little sailboat sideways. The boom came crashing across. Luckily Ryan and Kendra were crouched down in the boat, trying to hang on, and the boom whistled harmlessly over their heads. *Pegasus* wobbled back and forth a few times but the waves passed and things were calm again.

Claire looked furious. "What an idiot!" she fumed. "He was trying to swamp us! And laughing about it! Did anyone see the name of the boat?" But nobody had - everyone was too busy trying to hang on!

They sailed slowly the rest of the way back to Pirate Cove, with Kendra bailing out the water that had come over the side when the waves hit them. As they came close to shore they could see Nathan was already in the water, floating about on an air mattress. He waved as they sailed by. As soon as *Pegasus* was tied up at the dock, the three others leaped into the water to join him. Claire swam quickly over to Nathan and tipped over the air mattress, sending Nathan into the water.

"No fair!" he cried, spluttering as he came up. He tried to grab hold of the air mattress but Claire was already paddling away on it. He tried to swim after her but Claire was too fast and soon put some distance between them.

"Help me, you two!" he shouted to Kendra and Ryan. The two of them hesitated a moment, then began to swim in the direction of the air mattress. Seeing them coming, Claire set off again, this time kicking with her feet. Ryan soon gave up but Kendra kept going, swimming in strong steady strokes. She passed Nathan and in no time had caught Claire and flipped her into the water.

"Is that all the gratitude I get for giving you sailing lessons?" said Claire, laughing as she wiped the water from her eyes. By now Nathan had caught up and was clambering back onto the air mattress. The children continued to push one and other off the air mattress, hooting and hollering without stop. The water was cool and refreshing and the hot sun beat down on them as they swam. After a while Kendra and Nathan swam back to shore, leaving Claire floating alone. Ryan was already on the dock, sitting in a deck chair reading a book with Meg curled up at his feet.

They spent a lazy afternoon at the beach, jumping back in the water whenever it got too hot. Ryan wandered the length of the bay collecting sea shells and poking under rocks to see what he could find. Nathan and Kendra decided to build a sandcastle and Nathan found some buckets and spades in the boathouse. The sand was excellent for sandcastles, not too dry and not too wet. Soon an enormous castle had been built, decorated with rocks, shells, and seaweed. But the incoming tide meant a never ending effort to repair walls and fortifications as the waves wore them away. As the sun got lower in the sky their stomachs began to rumble. Suddenly, a bell clanged.

"Dinnertime!" said Nathan. They put away their things and Claire pulled *Pegasus* up on one side of the dock. Then they hurried up the path to the house as they were all feeling very hungry by this time.

"Dinner's almost ready," said Aunt Jennie as they came in the door. "Could you set the table, please? We'll eat outside since it's such a beautiful day."

Nathan and Ryan gathered dishes and cutlery and carried them to the patio. Outside, Uncle William was standing by the barbecue, enveloped in a huge cloud of smoke. Occasionally a huge flame leaped up from the barbecue. Finally, he gave a cry of victory and slamming the barbecue lid down, strode over to the table with an enormous platter of hamburger patties.

"Perfect," he declared as he set the platter on the table.

The four children munched happily on their burgers as their aunt and uncle enquired about their afternoon. Uncle William laughed when he heard about Kendra getting knocked overboard. "Happens to the best of us," he said with a smile. But he frowned and looked concerned upon hearing about the boat that nearly swamped them.

"Well, not nearly so much excitement up here," said Aunt Jennie. "William spent the afternoon working on his secret project."

"What secret project?" asked Ryan.

"Oh, he won't tell you," said Claire. "He's been all smug and secretive about it for weeks and won't even give us a hint. He just locks himself in his workshop and clatters about, making lots of noise."

"Now, now, all will be revealed when the time is right," said her father, looking mysterious.

"All right, who's for dessert?" asked Aunt Jennie. She went into the kitchen and came back with a large rhubarb cake. "Fresh rhubarb from the garden," she said proudly. She dished a piece out to each of them, topped with vanilla ice cream.

As they were finishing dessert, Aunt Jennie exclaimed, "I almost forgot, there was some exciting news in the village today. A humpback whale has been spotted in the channel!" Everyone turned and stared at her, even Uncle William. "Yes, a whale has been seen a number of times and it's been confirmed by some of the local fishermen. Apparently, it's the first humpback whale sighting in these parts in nearly a hundred years. Imagine! Humpbacks used to be quite common but commercial whaling nearly wiped them out."

"Will we be able to see it?" asked Ryan excitedly. He loved animals and a chance to see a whale in the wild would be a dream come true.

"Well, if it sticks around I suppose we've all got a chance of seeing it," said Aunt Jennie. "Keep your eyes open!"

* * *

The next day dawned bright and sunny. Kendra awoke early, unused to the bright sun shining through the window. Claire was still sleeping so she got dressed quietly and made her way down the hallway. Aunt Jennie was already up and in the kitchen.

"Good morning," said her aunt. "Did you sleep well?"

"Yes, thank you," replied Kendra. She had slept

with the window wide open and had drifted off to sleep with the scent of cedar trees in her head. Rarely had she slept so deeply. "May I help with anything?" she asked.

Aunt Jennie was pouring flour into a large bowl. "You could cook up those sausages if you don't mind," she said, pointing to a large pile of sausages on a plate. "We're having blueberry pancakes for breakfast. I hope you like blueberries."

"Oh yes!" said Kendra, eyeing up the tub of blueberries in front of her aunt. The two of them worked together in the kitchen while Aunt Jenny told her about her work as a councillor and various goings on in the community. After a while Nathan wandered in, rubbing his head and looking half asleep.

"Mmm, pancakes," he said as he popped a couple of blueberries into his mouth. Soon the others were up and they sat down to the delicious breakfast that Kendra and Aunt Jenny had put together. After breakfast everyone helped wash up and then changed into their swimsuits. Aunt Jenny made them some sandwiches which they packed in a cooler with some snacks and drinks. That way they could spend the whole day at the beach without the need to come back for lunch.

At the beach, the sun was just coming up over the bluff. The wet sand sparkled where the tide had recently gone out. A light breeze rippled the waters of the bay. Ryan was eager for more sailing lessons so they launched *Pegasus* and put up the sail. Claire showed them how to sail at different directions to the wind and adjust the sail accordingly. Ryan and Kendra took turns steering *Pegasus* around the bay. Claire was very impressed by how quickly Ryan had grasped the key principles of sailing. He could read the wind and position the sail almost as well as she could. Kendra was also starting to figure things out, although she still turned the tiller the wrong way on occasion.

Later Nathan switched places with Claire. Nathan was not as accomplished a sailor as his sister but he had spent plenty of time sailing around the bay and had no trouble handling the little boat by himself.

When they tired of sailing they brought *Pegasus* back to shore and tied up to the dock. Then they all went for a swim, as the sun was high in the sky now and the day was getting hot. Afterwards, they lay on the dock sunning themselves.

"So when are we going to start searching for the treasure?" asked Kendra. She had had trouble falling asleep the night before, thinking about the sunken wreck and wondering if it could be found. They knew the name of the boat and that its life ring had been found on a nearby beach. They also knew it had been stolen the night of a big storm and that the thieves were rumoured to have hit a rock. But that didn't seem like much information to go on.

"Well," said Claire slowly. "First we'll have to figure out where to look." She got up and went over to *Pegasus*. Opening a hatch on the front deck, she reached in and took out a clear sealed pouch. Inside were various charts and papers. Returning to the others, she pulled out a chart and spread it on the dock in front of them. "Get off Meg!" she said, pushing away the dog who had stepped onto the chart to investigate.

"We are here," she said, pointing to a small bay on the map. The name Rainy Bay had been crossed out and Pirate Cove written neatly in block letters. "Dad said the life ring was found on Hackett Beach, which is here." She pointed to a spot a little way down the coast from where they were. "So we should probably go there and start looking around."

Ryan looked at the chart. "That's the plan?" he said. "Shouldn't we narrow things down a bit more?"

"How?"

"Well, maybe we could find out which way the tide was going and the wind direction that night," he said. "And where on the beach the life ring was found. Then we could narrow down the search area."

"How would we find that out?" asked Nathan.

"We could look it up in the newspaper," said Claire. "There was probably an article about it. The library keeps old copies."

"The tide and weather information we can find on the Internet," said Ryan. "We can use your parents' computer."

Claire and Nathan looked at him and laughed. "You won't find one in our house," Claire said. "Mom and Dad wouldn't know how to switch it on. But there are a couple of computers at the library. We can ride our bikes into the village and visit the library."

"And buy some ice cream!" added Nathan. "They've got the best ice cream in the world at the store in the village!"

~ 5 ~

Tides and Wind

The next day they intended to ride into town, but Uncle William had other plans for them.

"I'm building a new fence for the vegetable garden and I need some help," he said. "A bear knocked a hole in the old one and if we don't get a new fence up soon the deer will eat everything in sight."

Nathan groaned, but Ryan and Kendra were happy to help. They didn't get to do many projects like that at home. Uncle William had them dig holes for the posts while he mixed concrete to make the footings. Then they helped pour the concrete and cut fence boards to length. The project took most of the morning.

"That looks good. We'll let the concrete set and in a few days we'll put the fence up," said Uncle William, wiping his brow. The sun was high overhead and had been beating down on them as they worked.

In exchange for their help that morning, Uncle William pulled some old bikes out of the shed after lunch. They were old and rusty and missing some parts, but still serviceable. He helped Kendra and Ryan pump up the tires and adjust the gears and brakes until the bikes were ready to use.

"They're not much to look at but they should get

you into town," he said when the work was finished.

Digging around in the shed, Kendra found an old basket and attached it to the front of her bike. "Now I've got something to carry my things in," she said, pleased with her handiwork.

By this time it was too late in the afternoon to cycle into town, so they spent the rest of the day swimming and playing on the beach. The next morning they would cycle into Maple Harbour.

* * *

The following day they set off on their bicycles on a trail through the woods. It was only a few kilometres to the village and the ride through the tall fir trees was pleasant and cool. After a while, the trail rejoined the main road and led them to the centre of Maple Harbour. They parked their bikes in front of the library, which was a small wooden building with clapboard siding. Kendra and Ryan looked at each other and grinned; it was probably one-tenth the size of their library at home.

Inside, the librarian showed them where they could find old copies of the *Coast Gazette*, the local newspaper which was published once a week. Uncle William had told them the boat had sunk sometime in August three years ago, so they gathered all the copies for that month and spread them out on a table. Each of them took a copy and began to flip through the pages, looking for any references to the event.

"Got it!" cried Nathan after a short while. Everyone crowded round to see. Nathan read the article aloud:

Big Storm Lashes the Coast

An unexpected summer storm caught residents off guard on Wednesday night, with damage reported to several boats and docks. Winds reaching 120 km/h were reported with five-metre waves. Several boats at Hudson's Marina received minor damage and Mr. Bert Richards reported that part of his floating dock had detached and broken up on shore. Mrs. Betty Simpson discovered a life ring on Hackett Beach early Thursday morning belonging to the motorboat Gypsy Moth. The Gypsy Moth was reported as stolen by its owner, Chad Hawkins, but there has been no sign of the vessel. Search and Rescue have had no reported injuries or fatalities.

"This paper is dated Friday, August 11th," said Claire, looking at the front cover. "So the storm was on August 9th."

"Do you know Betty Simpson?" said Ryan. "We could ask her where the life ring was found."

"Yes, she's an old lady that walks the beach each morning collecting things that wash up on shore," replied Claire. "Her house is on Hackett Beach, just a little way off the road to our house."

"Maybe we can visit her on the way home," said Kendra.

"Yes, we should be able to do that," agreed Claire. "Assuming she's home."

"All right, let's look up the winds and tides for that night," said Ryan, looking about for a computer. One of the two computers was free and they gathered around while Claire logged in with her library card. She searched for the weather office and then clicked on the historical weather data.

"We'll have to use the lighthouse at Point Hutchinson," she said. "The village doesn't have a weather station." She brought up the results for Point Hutchinson and paged through them until she came to August three years previous.

"It says that winds were light until just after midnight," she said, looking at the table of data on the screen. "Then it picked up, reaching 70 km/h at 3:00 a.m. That's the average speed," she added, "so the 120 km/h mentioned in the paper was probably just occasional gusts. It looks like the storm died down by 6:00

a.m. Wind direction was fairly steady from the southwest. That's unusual around here though; most of our storms come from the northwest."

"What about the tides?" said Ryan.

Claire exited the weather site and searched for tide tables. Finding one, she entered the date of the storm.

"Low tide was at 11:15 p.m. High tide was at 5:25 a.m. That means the tide was coming in, so it would have been in the same general direction as the wind. It was a fairly large tide too, so there would have been a good current."

"And with high tide at 5:25 a.m., the life ring would have washed up and been left on the beach just before Betty Simpson came along in the morning, right?" said Ryan.

"That's right," nodded Claire.

"Let's go find Betty Simpson!" said Kendra excitedly.

"Wait! Not until I've had my ice cream," put in Nathan.

Claire wrote down the details of the weather and tides, while Ryan made a photocopy of the newspaper article. Afterwards, the four walked down the street to the ice cream shop. Inside there was a wide array of flavours, from Triple Chocolate to Salmonberry.

"What's a Salmonberry?" asked Kendra.

"It's a like a blackberry, except orange," explained

Nathan. "They grow around here in early summer. They're delicious."

"They're a bit sour," warned Claire. "Nathan likes them, but I'm not sure they would make the best ice cream flavour."

They each ordered a cone and took them outside. The ice cream was rich and creamy. Kendra thought that it was indeed the best in the world as Nathan had claimed. They sat licking their cones on a bench outside the store, going over what they'd learned in the library.

"So we know the life ring was found on Hackett Beach," said Claire. "And the wind was from the southwest."

"And the tide was coming in," added Ryan. "So if Betty Simpson can tell us where she found the life ring we should have a good idea where to search."

As they spoke a police car drove up and parked in front of them. A tall, dark-haired police officer got out and gave them a wave.

"That's Sergeant Sandhu," said Nathan. "He's a friend of Dad's."

"Hi kids," said the officer, walking up to them. "Enjoying the summer holidays?"

The children nodded their heads. Claire introduced Ryan and Kendra and he shook hands with each of them.

"Another busy day fighting crime?" asked Claire with a smile. There was rarely any crime in Maple Harbour more serious than poaching crab traps.

"Well, Mrs. Dougall's poodle escaped again. Let's hope someone finds it before the coyotes do. And Stan Hodgson reported a ladder being stolen, but I suspect he just forgot where he left it."

Then his face clouded over. "Actually, we have had something more serious occur." He hesitated. "I suppose I can tell you, it will be in the paper this week anyway. You know the Thompson House?"

Claire nodded. "It's the most incredible house," she said looking at Ryan and Kendra. "It's located on a rocky island and is all concrete and glass. The living room sticks out right over the water."

"That's the one," he said. "It was designed by a famous architect decades ago as a summer home for a lumber baron. Now it's owned by Steven Chang, who started an Internet company and sold it for millions. What most people don't know is that Mr. Chang is an avid collector of Pacific Northwest art. He has a collection worth millions, including some well known pieces by Emily Carr, E.J. Hughes, and Jeff Wall. Or perhaps I should say had, because last week his house was broken into and much of the collection was stolen."

"Wow! Didn't he have a security system?" asked

Ryan.

"Yes, quite a sophisticated one. But the thieves managed to bypass it."

"Do you have any leads?" asked Kendra.

"Not so far. It's pretty hard to sell art like that. They may be part of a larger international gang who find buyers for it overseas. So we're waiting for them to make a move."

"We'll keep our eyes open," promised Claire. "And let you know if we see anything."

Sergeant Sandhu left them and walked up the street. The four children looked at each other.

"Wow!" said Nathan. "Art thieves in Maple Harbour. Imagine that!"

* * *

The children finished their ice cream and walked back to their bikes.

The day was considerably warmer now and they were soon wiping the perspiration from their brows as they pedalled along the road. They came to the turnoff that led to Hackett Beach and Betty Simpson's house and were relieved to be cycling through the cool forest again. Just before the beach, they came to a ramshackle house hidden in the trees. The children leaned their bikes against the rickety fence and pushed through an old gate that was latched with a frayed piece of yellow rope.

A large veranda encircled the house, and the railing was covered with artifacts collected from the beach. Some were real treasures, such as glass fishing floats and colourful old bottles. But much of it appeared to be junk—tires, blocks of broken Styrofoam, and unidentifiable pieces of rusted metal. There were also numerous shells and skeletons of dead sea creatures. At the top of the steps leading to the veranda, the skull of a sea lion glared down at them. Kendra shuddered involuntarily as she followed the others up the steps.

As Claire was about to ring the bell, there was a ferocious barking behind them. They all turned at once. Charging toward them was a huge black dog, with its fur bristling and its teeth bared!

6

Uncle William's Invention

Just as the dog reached the bottom of the steps the door opened and there was a sharp whistle. The dog stopped in its tracks and immediately sat down. An old woman in a faded calico dress stood in the doorway.

"I'm so sorry," she said. "We don't get many visitors, and old Charlie can be a bit overprotective. Now what can I do for you?"

"Hello, Mrs. Simpson," said Claire, glancing nervously back at the dog. "I'm Claire Daniels. This is my brother Nathan and our cousins Ryan and Kendra. We live just up the road."

"Oh yes, I remember you when you were a little girl. And your brother. But I haven't seen much of you lately. Although I don't get out as much as I used to. Come on in." She turned back into the house and the children followed her. The inside of the house was even spookier than outside, with more beach artifacts and skeletons, some of them mounted on pieces of gnarled driftwood. She led them through the house and indicated an old sofa to sit on, which sagged under their weight.

"Now, what brings you here today?"

Claire explained their hunt for the sunken wreck

and how they had read about the discovery of the *Gypsy Moth's* life ring in the newspaper.

"Oh yes, I remember that storm." She laughed softly. "One of the worst I've ever seen here in the summertime. It was more like the worst of the winter storms. I knew there would be a good chance of finding things washed up on shore the next morning so I went out early. But all I found was that life ring and some plastic bottles, if I remember correctly."

"Where did you find the life ring?" interrupted Kendra impatiently. Ryan glared at her but old Mrs. Simpson just smiled.

"Eager to get on with your search, are you? Well, I found it at the far end of Hackett Beach, just by the old water tank. The tide was just starting to go out again and it had been left at the high tide line."

After chatting a bit more, Claire thanked her for the information and made to leave.

"Do you want to see it?" The children looked surprised and nodded eagerly. The old woman went into a back room. She came out carrying a white life ring with orange stripes around it. On it, the words *Gypsy Moth* could be clearly seen written along the side. They stared at it for a while, until Mrs. Simpson put it back and showed them to the door.

"Have you seen the whale?" she asked as they were leaving. They shook their heads.

"It was by here this morning. I saw it spout just off Hackett Beach. It's certainly a magnificent sight. Keep your eyes peeled and I'm sure you'll see it."

* * *

By the time they arrived home it was almost supper time. Uncle William was just coming out of his workshop as they rode in and he gave them a wave.

"Did you find out what you needed?" he asked.

"We found the tide and wind information at the library," answered Ryan. "And we went to visit Betty Simpson, who discovered the life ring."

"Old Mrs. Simpson, well, well. I haven't seen her in years. She's become quite reclusive of late. Is she still in that old house of hers on Hackett Beach?"

"Yes, it's quite spooky," said Kendra. "But she was very nice and told us where she found the life ring. She even showed it to us."

"Uncle William, how's your secret project going?" asked Kendra, peering past him into the workshop.

"I'm glad you asked, Kendra, it's almost ready to go. In fact, I might unveil it for you after dinner."

Together they trooped into the house where Aunt Jennie was just pulling a big lasagna out of the oven."I hope everyone's hungry," she said.

The four children were all very hungry after their cycle into Maple Harbour and had soon finished two helpings each of lasagna. After dinner, they helped wash the dishes and then made their way to the workshop where Uncle William was just putting the final touches on his creation.

"All right, come on in," he said. They blinked as they entered, their eyes adjusting to the gloom of the workshop. Inside a large sheet covered up something on the edge of the workbench. Uncle William paused until their eyes had a chance to adjust to the light and then he pulled the sheet off with a flourish. "Ta da!"

The four of them stared. Mounted on the edge of the bench was an old boat motor, connected to a fuel tank.

"It's just a boat motor," said Nathan after a moment's silence.

"Yes, but it's a *special* boat motor," said his father proudly. "I've adapted it to run on used cooking oil. So it's free to operate and it's much better for the environment."

"I didn't know you had a boat," said Ryan.

"I don't. But I thought we could use it on *Pegasus*."

"You will not!" said Claire, a horrified look on her face.

Her father was momentarily taken aback but quickly recovered. "Well, maybe I'll get myself a small boat. Anyway, it's time for the demonstration." The children watched in silence as he put a plastic garbage can under the propeller shaft and filled it with water from a garden hose. Next, he filled the fuel tank with a dark yellow oil from a large pop bottle he took from a shelf.

"That's the cooking oil," he said. "Now we're ready to fire it up." Uncle William flicked a switch and rotated the throttle. Then he took the starter cord and gave it a hard pull. Nothing happened. He adjusted the choke and pulled the starter cord again. Still nothing happened. He pulled a third time and the engine came to life with a roar.

Uncle William beamed at them. Kendra and Ryan applauded, while Nathan and Claire just stared at the motor dubiously. Meg ran out of the room as soon as the engine started.

"What's that smell?" asked Nathan. A smell of stale French fries had begun to fill the room.

"That's the cooking oil. It always gives off a bit of a French fry smell when it burns."

Suddenly the engine began to splutter and a thin stream of black smoke started to pour out the top. Uncle William reached over to turn it off, but as he did there was a shower of sparks. A sheet of flame shot out of the engine cowling.

"Get out!" yelled Uncle William. "Get out!"

7

The Search Begins

The four children needed no further encouragement and ran through the door. As they turned back to look there was a loud bang, followed by silence. Uncle William peeked in the door and cautiously went in. He grabbed a fire extinguisher from the wall and sprayed it on the flames that were coming out of the engine. Once the fire was out they all surveyed the damage. The engine was a mess of blackened metal and melted plastic.

"I'm sorry, Uncle William," said Kendra, feeling badly for her uncle.

"Oh well, I didn't have a boat to use it on anyway," her uncle replied, shaking his head sadly. "I'm just glad nobody got hurt. Maybe don't mention this to your mother," he added with a knowing look at Claire and Nathan. They rolled their eyes but grudgingly agreed.

After helping Uncle William clean up, they returned to the house to plan the next day's expedition. They would wear their swimsuits but would need towels and a change of clothes in case it got cold. Masks, snorkels, and fins would be needed for diving. Claire folded her chart and put it inside a plastic ziplock bag to keep it dry, along with her compass and a black felt pen.

"We'll bring the anchor with us tomorrow," she said. "I don't usually carry it because it's so heavy, but we may need to anchor while we're swimming around looking for the wreck."

"What about a rope and a float to mark the spot once we've found it?" asked Ryan.

"That's a good idea. I've got some rope in the boathouse and we can take a plastic bottle out of the recycling. We can also bring some light rope and a weight to use as a depth sounder."

"Don't forget we'll need lots of food," added Nathan. "Treasure hunting is hungry work, I'm sure!"

With their plans made, the four children retired to bed, eager for the morning to arrive. Tomorrow they might find a sunken wreck!

* * *

The next morning everyone was up early. They wolfed down their breakfast and quickly packed up some ham sandwiches for lunch. They were just heading out the door when Aunt Jennie entered the kitchen wearing her housecoat.

"I see you're eager to get going. Have you packed a good lunch?" Nathan held up the large bag holding their lunch and nodded.

"Be careful out there. The weather report says that the wind may pick up this afternoon. Claire, you're the captain and responsible for this motley crew."

"Of course." Claire gave her mother a kiss on the cheek and, hoisting her bag over her shoulder, disappeared out the door with a wave, followed by the others. Her mother watched them go, a smile on her face. She knew she could trust Claire. Not only was Claire an excellent sailor, but she was very level-headed and responsible.

Down on the dock, they loaded their gear into *Pegasus* and pushed the boat into the water. Meg was left behind as it would be too long a day for her to spend in the boat. She sat on the dock watching them mournfully. There was a very light breeze, just enough to fill the sail and keep them moving through the water. They tacked out of the bay and into the open water. Down the coast they could see Hackett Beach. The tide was out and the sand reflected brightly in the early morning sun. Claire pointed the bow downwind and sailed toward the end of Hackett Beach. As they got closer the wind dropped until it died completely and the sail hung limply from the mast. Claire looked at it in disgust.

"There goes our wind," she grumbled.

"Maybe that's best," said Ryan. "It would be pretty hard to search while tacking back and forth. Why don't a couple of us put the masks and snorkels on and start swimming while the other two paddle along in the boat."

"Okay, that sounds like a good plan." Claire hated to be in a sailboat with no wind, but she could see Ryan's point. She pulled out her chart.

"Now if the *Gypsy Moth* hit a rock, it would need to be here at Fulsom Point." She pointed at a piece of land jutting out a little way south of Hackett Beach. "That's the only spot where there are rocks in this area, other than right up on the beach. And it would fit with where the life ring was found. So let's start swimming here and work our way as far as Fulsom Point. Who wants to start snorkelling?"

"I do!" said Kendra. "I'm already roasting."

"I will too," said Ryan. He was eager to be the one to find the sunken boat, and with snorkel and fins his sister didn't have such an advantage over him in the water.

The two of them pulled off their t-shirts and sandals and put on the snorkelling gear while Claire dropped the sail into the boat. Ryan jumped off the boat with a great splash, followed by Kendra. Nathan howled in protest as a sheet of water caught him in the face.

Ryan and Kendra put their heads down and began swimming, one on either side of the boat. Claire and Nathan could hear their heavy breathing through the snorkels. Claire kept *Pegasus* moving by sculling with the rudder, waggling it back and forth, while Nathan lay with his head over the bow, peering into the greeny-blue depths.

Claire looked at her chart. The water depth was about 7 metres. Further out it got gradually deeper, reaching a depth of 25 metres before suddenly dropping off to well over 100. She knew if the *Gypsy Moth* sank beyond that point there would be no chance of finding it. And it couldn't be further in or it would show at low tide. So that left an area about 100 metres wide and nearly a kilometre long to search. It was a lot to cover, she thought to herself, but Ryan and Kendra were making good speed with their fins.

They made their way down the coast to Fulsom Point. Claire aimed *Pegasus* at a tree on the tip of the point and every so often she would give a yell to Kendra and Ryan to adjust their direction. Nathan soon got bored of looking over the bow as he could see very little, and he pulled out a book to read.

After 20 minutes or so they reached Fulsom Point and turned around. Then they swam back the way they had come, slightly further out. They were nearly back where they had started when Kendra gave a muffled shout through her snorkel. She waved her hand in the air. Claire stopped sculling and looked over the side.

"What do you see?" Nathan shouted.

Kendra popped her head out of the water and

pulled the snorkel from her mouth. "I'm not sure," she said, "but it's some type of equipment."

"Is it a boat?"

"No, but it might be part of a boat. It's partly submerged in the silt on the bottom."

"Can you swim down to it?" asked Claire.

"I think so."

"Here, take this rope. It's got a hook on the end. See if you can hook it on and we can pull it up." She handed Kendra the rope.

Kendra took the rope from her, gripping the hook in her right hand. She put her snorkel back in her mouth and floated face down for a few seconds. Taking a big breath of air, she kicked her feet up and dove down toward the bottom. Nathan could see her orange fins clearly even as the rest of her disappeared into the gloom of the deep water. Claire payed out the rope as Kendra pulled on it, keeping it taut to prevent it from tangling. After what seemed like ages, but was probably only 15 or 20 seconds, she burst back through the surface, pulling the snorkel from her mouth and taking big gulps of air.

"It's on!" she said between breaths.

Claire began to pull on the rope. Whatever it was, it was very heavy and didn't seem to want to budge. Nathan came over to help and Ryan, pulling his mask and fins off, clambered into the boat to assist them.

Together they heaved on the line and felt it give. Another heave and it moved some more.

"It's stuck in the mud, but I think it's coming loose!" said Claire. "Okay, one, two, three..." They gave another great pull and the rope suddenly came free, sending the three of them sprawling backwards.

"What happened?" asked Kendra, who was treading water beside the boat.

"The hook must have come loose." Ryan glared at his sister, rubbing his backside where he'd landed on the boat. Claire pulled the rope up and handed the hook end back to Kendra. She took it and again dove down to the sea bottom. A few moments later she was back at the surface.

"I wrapped it around a few times so it won't come off this time," she said.

The others took hold of the rope again and began to pull. This time it was easier and they didn't have to give such great heaves. The rope came in steadily, hand over hand. Soon, the object was rising toward them. As it broke the surface they stopped pulling and looked over the side eagerly. Then their faces dropped.

"What is it?" asked Kendra.

"It's a... a lawnmower," answered Nathan and he started to laugh. "It's an old lawnmower, the push kind. And it's very rusty. I don't think it has cut any lawns for a long time."

Kendra looked incredulous. "A lawnmower? Really? What's a lawnmower doing in the ocean?"

"You find all kinds of things in the ocean," said Claire. "Sometimes they fall off ships or get washed off the shore. Other times people just toss things, using it as a sort of garbage dump." She unhooked the rope, taking care not to cut herself on the sharp rusty edges. She let the lawnmower slip back into the water, watching it disappear into the murky depths. She didn't like to leave it there, but there was no way to get it into *Pegasus* and bring it back with them.

Kendra climbed back on board and Nathan pulled out some snacks to eat. It was nice to feel the warm sun, Kendra thought, after all that time in the water. Although the water was quite warm for the west coast, she still felt chilled after spending so much time in it.

Once the snacks had been eaten Claire and Nathan put on the snorkeling gear while Kendra and Ryan remained in the boat. Claire showed Ryan how to scull with the rudder and which areas had already been covered. They continued their search, slowly swimming back and forth in long lines, slightly further from shore each time. But there were no more shouts of discovery from the swimmers. As the water got deeper Kendra could see less and less looking over the bow.

At last, they reached the point where the sea bottom dropped off. Beyond that the water was dark and nothing could be seen at all. They finished searching along the line of the underwater cliff until they reached Fulsom Point. Claire and Nathan climbed back on board *Pegasus*.

"That's the whole area," said Claire, her voice tinged with disappointment. "I guess we won't find the wreck after all."

Kendra looked at her in disbelief. She had been so excited about the possibility of discovering a sunken wreck, she couldn't accept that the search was over already. She didn't really expect to find any treasure but had sincerely believed they would find the boat.

"We can't give up yet," she said. "Real treasure hunters spend years looking for wrecks. We've only been looking for a few hours."

"Yes, but these are the only rocks that it could have hit in this area," said Claire. "So it must have gone down in the deep part, past the dropoff. There's no way we can find it there."

"Are you sure these are the only rocks?" asked Ryan.

"Here, you can check it yourself," she said, handing him the chart.

Ryan spread out the chart on the bow deck and poured over it while the others pulled out the sandwiches and began to eat. The wind had begun to pick up again and *Pegasus* was slowly drifting toward shore. Nathan pulled the anchor out of the front hatch where it had been stored and dropped it overboard with a splash. He felt it hit the bottom and gave a tug to make sure it was secure. They ate their lunch in silence, with only the sound of the waves lapping gently at the bow.

After a while Ryan spoke up. "What about this shallow bit out here?" he said. He pointed to a spot on the chart further out and to the south. Claire looked over his shoulder.

"It's shallow, but it's still three metres deep. A boat couldn't have hit that, even at low tide."

"But didn't you say the tide was very low that night"

"Yes, let me check." She pulled out her notes from their day at the library. "Wow, you're right, it was only 0.2 metres! That's about as low as it gets."

"What difference would that make?" asked Nathan.

"With the storm there would have been big waves," said Ryan. "So if the boat was at the bottom of a wave it would actually be lower than what the tide table says. Right Claire?"

Claire thought about it for a second. "I suppose so. If they were crossing exactly at low tide."

"It fits with what your father said, the rumour that whoever stole the boat hit some 'unexpected' rocks. You would think the thieves would know all the rocks and shallows around here, wouldn't you? Maybe they thought they could cross here but didn't realize it wasn't safe with the combination of the storm and the unusually low tide that night."

"That's a possibility," said Claire, looking interested again. "Gee, you sure know a lot about tides for a landlubber," she added with a laugh. "All right, who's up for exploring further out?" Kendra shouted "Hooray!" in agreement, while Nathan, whose mouth was full of sandwich, gave a thumbs up.

The sail was raised again and the anchor pulled up. The breeze was picking up and *Pegasus* surged through the water, seemingly eager to explore this new region.

Soon they were well out in the strait. The wind was quite strong, heeling the little boat over on its side even with four of them in it. The sun was still shining but much of the sky had filled with clouds. Claire kept glancing to the south where tall dark storm clouds were ominously building. She had a worried look on her face.

"What are you thinking?" Ryan asked, glancing toward her. As he spoke a jagged bolt of lightning flashed in the distance and there was a low rumble of thunder.

"There's a storm coming," she answered slowly. "And it looks like a bad one! I think we'd better turn back." As she spoke a hard gust of wind hit *Pegasus*, tipping it sharply.

"Good idea," said Nathan, who was definitely a fair

weather sailor.

Claire turned the boat around and pointed back toward Pirate Cove. With the wind behind them the boat flew along, surfing on the waves. Every so often gusts would knock them one way or the other and Claire struggled to keep them on course.

"Keep your heads down! It will be no joke if you get hit by the boom in this wind!" She had to yell now to be heard, with the wind whistling in their ears.

There were claps of thunder behind them and jagged flashes of lightning against the dark sky. Ryan looked at the flashes nervously. Being in a small boat with a metal mast in a lightning storm sounded like a bad idea, he thought. The wind was blowing spray from the top of the waves, drenching them in cold water. What a change from that morning, when they had been far too hot!

Suddenly a strong gust hit them as they were cresting a wave. The boat tipped over until the edge of the sail was dragging in the water. It hung precariously on its side, about to topple over!

Suddenly a strong gust hit them.

8

Whalebone Island

Claire flung herself over the opposite side, leaning out as far as she could to bring *Pegasus* back to rights. The others scrambled to do the same. Slowly the boat righted itself and almost immediately the sail filled again as they were carried over the next wave.

Water was sloshing around in the bottom of the boat and Nathan began to bail frantically, but more came over the side with each new wave that struck them. Kendra and Ryan gripped the side of the boat as tightly as possible, their knuckles turning white.

"Hang on tight, we're going to turn!" Claire shouted. "Keep your heads down!" She turned the tiller and rapidly pulled in the sail as *Pegasus* turned through the wind. The boom swung over their heads and Claire let the sail out again as they took off in the opposite direction.

"Where are you going?" yelled Ryan, trying to be heard over the howling wind.

"Over there!" Claire pointed ahead, where there was the outline of a small island. "There's a small cove where I think we can find shelter!" The island was about a kilometre away but they covered the distance quickly. As they came around the leeward side of the island the wind dropped and *Pegasus* slowed down, the mast straightening. Although the wind was still fairly strong, it seemed peaceful compared to the full force of the storm. The calm didn't last, however, as they soon emerged on the other side of the island where the wind picked up again. But Claire turned into the wind and soon a small cove appeared in front of them.

"Keep an eye out for rocks!" Claire commanded. "I think it's clear but I don't know for sure." She aimed for the middle of the cove, easing the sail out to slow them down. The others peered into the water ahead of them, while Nathan picked up an oar and held it out, ready to fend off any rocks that should appear. But the way was clear and soon the wind dropped once more as they entered the cove. A moment later the boat landed gently on a pebbly beach. Kendra and Nathan hopped out and pulled *Pegasus* up out of the water.

Ryan looked over at Claire. "Nice job," he said. "It's a good thing you knew about this place."

"Thanks," she said. "I've never stopped here before but I've seen it on the chart and sailed past it once. With a north wind it wouldn't be as sheltered, but with this windstorm from the south it's a perfect place to stop."

"What's this island called?" asked Nathan.

"Whalebone Island. I'm not sure why, maybe a big

whalebone was found here once. There used to be commercial whaling around here a long time ago, with a whaling station on the other side of the strait. But people hunted the whales almost to extinction and they're pretty rare now."

"I know," groaned Kendra. "That's why I want to see the one in Maple Harbour!"

They looked around the little cove. It was no more than 20 metres across, with a small beach of fine pebbles. At the top of the beach lay a jumble of logs and driftwood piled high from winter storms. An old fishing net was wrapped around some of the logs at one end. Behind was a thick tangle of blackberry bushes, which ended at a steep rocky cliff rising above them. The cliff wrapped around the cove, creating rocky promontories on either side.

They plunked themselves down on a log and pulled out what remained of their food. There wasn't much, just a few granola bars and some apples, which were soon gone. In front of them, the windstorm continued to rage, although it was quite calm where they sat. However, the sound of thunder seemed to be getting farther away and there were no longer flashes of lightning. The children, still wearing their swimsuits, were quite chilled from the soaking they had received in the storm so they each put on a sweater.

"It's a good thing we brought these," said Kendra.

"I'd never have thought we'd need them this morning."
The others nodded in agreement, shivering.

"Do we have any more food?" asked Nathan, looking hungry.

"You just ate the last apple," replied Claire. "You
could look for some blackberries."

Nathan stood up and clambered over the piles of
driftwood to the sprawling blackberry bush behind
them. Kendra joined him and the two of them were
soon gorging themselves on the plump, sweet ber-
ries. Claire and Ryan sat in silence watching the waves
crash against the rocks on the side of the cove. The
wind whistled in the trees above them, punctuated by
the occasional yelp from Nathan and Kendra as they
pricked themselves on the sharp blackberry thorns.

Suddenly Nathan gave a loud shout. Claire and
Ryan turned to look. There was no sign of either of
them, seemingly swallowed by the blackberry bush.

"There's a cave back here!" called Nathan. "A big
one!"

There was some thrashing about and they heard
Kendra's voice. "Wow, cool! Come and check this out!"

Claire and Ryan jumped up and hurried over the
logs to the blackberry bush. It took them a while to
find their way through the dense brambles, but at last
they reached Nathan and Kendra. In front of them
was the mouth of a cave. It was round with a flat bot-

tom and about the height of a tall man.

"It looks more like a tunnel than a cave," said Ryan. "It's too round to be natural and the floor is flat."

Looking inside, the tunnel went quite far back, disappearing into the dark.

"I tried going in a bit, but it was too dark. I kept tripping on rocks," said Nathan.

"Did we bring a flashlight?" asked Ryan.

"There's one in *Pegasus*," said Claire. She went back to the boat to get it, returning shortly with a small flashlight as well as a headlamp. Nathan took the flashlight and Kendra the headlamp. Together they made their way slowly into the tunnel. It was cool, with a faint musty smell that became stronger further in. After a few metres the tunnel began to descend and then turned to the right. Ryan looked behind them. He could no longer see the opening, only a faint light showed where they had come from.

Suddenly Nathan stopped and Kendra almost ran into him. She looked at where his flashlight was pointing. In front of them was a big wooden door. It was painted black and looked very solid. In the middle of the door was a white sign with red lettering:

DANGER
Abandoned Mine Shaft
Closed - No Trespassing

They looked at the sign in dismay.

"I guess we can't go any further," said Kendra. "That's too bad, I was hoping we'd go right under the island and come out on the other side." She looked around the tunnel, the beam from the headlamp following her, and saw something lying on the floor. She stepped over and picked it up, shining her headlamp on it.

"It's a chocolate bar wrapper," she said, "And it seems fairly new. Perhaps someone's been here recently."

Nathan went up to the door. On one side were heavy steel hinges. On the other was a solid steel clasp with a lock. The door and sign looked very old, but the lock and clasp were new and reflected brightly in the beam of his flashlight. He gave the door a push but it didn't budge.

After looking around some more, they turned back and returned to the mouth of the tunnel. Outside the storm had abated and the sun was beginning to poke out between the clouds.

"We'd better start back," said Claire. "Mom will be wondering where we are."

They pushed *Pegasus* back into the water and climbed aboard. The storm had died down, but the waves were as big as before and the boat rolled from side to side as it crested each wave. There was still a stiff breeze and soon they were within sight of Pirate Cove. Aunt Jennie and Uncle William were waving to them from the shore.

They nosed into the dock and Uncle William reached down and took the bow line. "Safe and sound I see."

"Of course," said Claire with a grin. "Did you have any doubts?"

"I didn't, but I think your mother might have."

"I didn't doubt your abilities, but they wouldn't help you much if you were struck by lightning," Aunt Jennie pointed out. "That was quite a storm. And regardless of what your father says, I think he was a bit worried too."

"Maybe just the teeniest bit," Uncle William admitted. "I was watching you from the point and I saw you change course to Whalebone Island, which was a good decision. So I figured you were okay after that. But what were you doing way out there? I thought you were looking for the wreck near Hackett Beach?"

The children excitedly recounted the day's adventures, describing their unsuccessful search, being caught in the storm, and finally, the old mine tunnel they had discovered.

"There was an old copper mine there many years ago, back in the late 1800's," said Uncle William. "But the copper didn't last long and the mine was soon abandoned. It had a second life during the Prohibition era, when alcohol was banned in the United States and it was used by smugglers as a storage depot for illegal liquor heading across the border. I'm not surprised the tunnel has been closed off; it would be pretty dangerous after all these years."

They pulled *Pegasus* up onto the dock and, gathering their things, climbed the path back to the house. Aunt Jennie had a big pot of soup on the stove, with fresh baked bread. It was good to have a hot meal as they were still quite chilled from being soaked in the storm.

"By the way, you missed the whale again," said Aunt Jennie as they were eating. "It came right into the harbour this morning. I was picking up some groceries and someone mentioned it was there. So I went down to the government wharf and there it was, not more than a hundred metres away!"

"Oh no," groaned Ryan. "And we were busy pulling up a lawnmower from the sea."

"I'm sure you'll get another chance to see it. It seems to be sticking around."

After dinner they sat on the back deck sucking on popsicles. The sky had cleared and the evening sun bathed the deck in a warm glow.

"These are very strange popsicles," said Ryan, holding his out in front of him.

"Mom puts all kinds of crazy things in them," said Nathan, catching a drip with his tongue. "Whatever fruits and vegetables she has handy. I think these are strawberry and zucchini."

"They are not!" said Claire, laughing and throwing a napkin at him. "She doesn't put zucchini in them!"

"She put kale in them once," protested Nathan.

"Only a tiny bit. And that was because you refuse to eat any vegetables."

"Well I think they taste good," said Kendra, jumping to her aunt's defense. She took another lick. "Are we going to go out treasure hunting again tomorrow?"

"Can't," said Claire. "I have a sailing race. Actually," she said, turning to Ryan, "I was wondering if you wanted to come along. As long as the wind isn't too light it would be good to have someone else to help out."

"Sure, sounds like fun," said Ryan. Secretly he was pleased that Claire would invite him. He knew she took her sailing quite seriously and he wasn't used to anyone wanting him on their team for a sporting activity.

"Great! Race is at 11:00 a.m. We'll have to leave here around 9:30 to sail into town and register."

"Can we come and watch?" asked Kendra.

"Of course. You and Nathan can ride your bikes there if you like and watch us from the government wharf. Bring the binoculars."

Nathan rolled his eyes. "You know that watching a sailing race is about as exciting as watching grass grow?"

"That's okay. I still want to watch them," said Kendra. "And maybe we'll see the whale!"

~ 9 ~

The Race

After a finishing a large breakfast of bacon and eggs the next morning, Claire and Ryan packed some water and snacks and left to sail *Pegasus* into Maple Harbour. Kendra went down to the dock to see them off.

"Good luck!" she called as they sailed away. "We'll be cheering for you." She waved at them until the little boat disappeared behind the rocky shore.

Out on the water *Pegasus* was making good progress toward Maple Harbour. The sky was filled with broken clouds and there was a stiff breeze from the south.

"Perfect weather for racing," said Claire. Ryan could see the anticipation on her face. He, on the other hand, felt butterflies in his stomach in spite of the breakfast he had just eaten. He was beginning to wish he had stayed home. What if he made a mistake that cost them the race? He hoped Claire wouldn't blame him if that happened. He couldn't be expected to know everything after only a few lessons, could he?

It took them about half an hour to sail into the village, leaving plenty of time before the race started. Claire guided *Pegasus* into the dock and hopped out, tying the boat up securely. They walked to shore and Claire led the way to an old wooden building with a number of flags flying in front of it. Inside, a friendly grey haired man with a bushy moustache and eyebrows to match was taking registrations for the race.

"Good morning Claire," he greeted her as they came in. "Fine day for racing."

"It sure is. This is my cousin Ryan, he's going to be racing with me today. This is George, he's in charge of the races," she said, introducing him to Ryan.

"Nice to meet you, Ryan," said George, holding out his hand. Ryan shook it, wincing a little as George squeezed his hand with a firm grip. "We've got a good turnout today, all the usual suspects."

"Which course are we sailing?" asked Claire.

"With this wind, I think we'll sail the long course. Down to the point, across to Pigeon Island, and back." Claire nodded.

After checking the tide tables, the two of them made their way back to the boat. As they were about to turn onto the dock there was a cry from the parking lot above.

"Hey, Claire! You sailing that bathtub of yours today?"

Ryan looked up. Two stocky boys with short blond hair were grinning down at them. Both were dressed in identical polo shirts and khaki shorts and carrying life jackets under their arms. He glanced at Claire, who rolled her eyes and looked away.

"I see you brought some ballast along," one of them sniggered. "Are you sure he meets the minimum height requirement?"

Ryan turned red, but Claire grabbed his arm and pulled him toward the dock. "Just ignore them," she muttered.

"Who are they?"

"The Mitchell brothers, Matthew and Flint. They're identical twins and identically obnoxious. They're good sailors but reckless. If there's ever a collision, the Mitchells are usually involved."

"Does that happen often?"

"No, but sometimes it does."

They reached *Pegasus,* climbed in, and cast off. Out in the bay there was a large red float with a white powerboat anchored a short distance away. A number of small sailboats were buzzing around in a chaotic fashion.

"That's the committee boat," said Claire, "and there's the first mark." She pointed at a yellow triangular float a long way down the shore. "The other mark is behind Pigeon Island so you can't see it. We have to start between the committee boat and the red mark, and then go around the other two marks counter-clockwise."

"So how does everyone avoid bumping into each other?"

"There are rules we have to follow. A boat on starboard tack has the right of way over one on port tack. Starboard tack means the wind is coming from the right hand side and your sail is on the left. Port tack is the opposite. The other important rule is that a downwind boat has right of way over an upwind boat. But you won't need to worry about that, I will. Right now, you just watch the time. Do you have a timer on your watch?"

Ryan nodded.

"Keep an eye on the committee boat. When it's five minutes until the start, a horn will sound and a flag will be put up. Start timing five minutes at that point. The flag will go down with one minute to go. It's really important we don't cross the line before the race starts or we'll have to start over."

Ryan set his watch to count down five minutes. There was still about 10 minutes until the race was scheduled to start. He watched the committee boat while Claire steered *Pegasus* back and forth a short distance from the start line. Suddenly a white flag was raised on the committee boat and a horn sounded. He pressed the start button on his watch and the seconds began to count down. The wind had picked up and they were moving quickly across the water. Claire had to tack back and forth frequently to avoid getting too far away from the start line. Suddenly another boat changed direction and cut right across their bow.

"Starboard!" cried a voice and Ryan saw the Mitchell brothers leering at them from the boat.

"Was that legal?" asked Ryan.

"Oh, yes. Just not very nice. They didn't give us much notice and there's no reason to be cutting in front of us like that with three minutes to go before the race starts."

"What did he yell 'Starboard' for?"

"That's to say that he is on starboard tack and has the right of way. It's a way of letting the other boat know that you're in danger of colliding and they expect you to change course and get out of their way. But with those two it's just a way of gloating."

Ryan glanced at his watch. "Two minutes," he said. He watched the other boats milling around. The Mitchells, after their encounter with *Pegasus*, had sailed quite a distance away and were now turning around to come back. The flag on the committee boat was suddenly lowered. One minute to go.

Now the other boats began to converge near the start line. Claire let the sail out, content to hover a short distance away. "Start counting down when we get to 30 seconds," she said.

At 30 seconds Claire pulled in the sail and turned

toward the start line, as others did the same. "20 seconds!" called out Ryan. Suddenly another boat appeared in front of them, blocking their wind, and *Pegasus* momentarily stalled. "10 seconds!" Ryan looked up and was alarmed to see the other boat only a few feet away. It was forcing Claire to turn up wind and sail straight toward the floating buoy that marked the start line. "Five seconds!" Claire desperately let out the sail, trying to slow their progress. But it was too late. She pushed the tiller hard and the boat turned with a jerk. As the sail clattered over his head Ryan heard the horn sound to start the race.

They had just missed hitting the buoy, but were now on the wrong side of it. They would have to turn around and start again. Claire looked grim as she made a circle and came back toward the start line. *Pegasus* was now well at the back, a substantial distance behind the other boats. Worst of all, the Mitchell brothers were out in front.

Ryan looked over at Claire, who gave him a sheepish grin. "Sorry, I messed that up. I shouldn't have tried to go so close to the start line."

"Is it hopeless for us?" he asked.

"We're not likely to win, but we can still have a good race. Let's see if we can catch up to some of these boats." Ryan relaxed a bit. He was happy to see that Claire wasn't taking it as hard as he thought she might. They settled down to playing catch-up.

As they tacked back and forth toward the point, Ryan looked at the houses along the shore. It was much more densely populated on this part of the coast. Some of the homes were small cottages, while others had been replaced by large houses. A few were perched on rocky cliffs where Ryan wouldn't have thought it was possible to build anything. He wondered what would happen to them if there was an earthquake. A few people stood on their decks watching the race through binoculars and one or two waved. Claire and Ryan waved back.

Just before the next floating mark they caught and passed the boat in front of them. An elderly man in a sailor's cap gave them a wave as they went by. He was smoking a pipe and didn't seem the least concerned about now being in last place.

"Ahoy there, Claire!" he called. "Not used to seeing you back here."

She shrugged her shoulders and smiled. "It happens."

They rounded the mark and set sail toward Pigeon Island, which was a long narrow island close to the opposite shore. Claire let Ryan set the sail while she steered for the next mark. People called out words of encouragement as they passed more boats. Claire was well liked by the other sailors and no one seemed surprised to be passed by her. By the time they rounded the next buoy they were in the middle of the pack, although the Mitchell brothers and a number of others were still ahead.

As they turned downwind, Pigeon Island lay straight ahead of them.

"Which way do we go?" asked Ryan.

"It's about the same distance either way," answered Claire, "but the inside channel doesn't usually have much wind." Ahead of them, all the other boats had gone to the outside of the island.

"I guess that's the way to go then."

"Mmm, I suppose so." Claire seemed undecided. She glanced behind her and suddenly turned *Pegasus* toward the inside channel. Ryan gave her a questioning look.

"Well, usually there's less wind, but sometimes it gets funnelled through the channel if the wind direction is right. And hey, we don't have anything to lose."

As they approached the channel they felt a rush of wind at their backs. "Hooray!" cried Ryan. "The wind is stronger here." The little boat surged through the channel, surfing on top of the waves. Emerging from the channel they could see that they had made up most of the distance between themselves and the boats in front.

"Let's stay on this side of the bay," said Claire. "We

can continue to benefit from this wind and then we'll head to the finish line on starboard tack." There was a wide smile on her face now and her eyes sparkled. Could they catch up to the other boats and win?

They continued in the same direction for another few minutes before turning toward the finish line. The other boats were also getting close to the line, with the Mitchell brothers still in front. As they got closer it appeared they were on a collision course with the Mitchells' boat. Ryan saw with dismay that the two boys were slightly ahead.

"They're going to win," he groaned.

"No they're not," said Claire determinedly. She kept *Pegasus* on a straight course, just inside the finish mark. The Mitchells held their course as well and it seemed a collision was imminent. But at the last moment Claire yelled "Starboard!" One of the Mitchells threw her an angry look before veering off sharply. Moments later the horn sounded and Claire threw her arms in the air. "That horn was for us," she said. "We won!"

~ 10 ~

Revenge!

When they got back on shore Kendra and Nathan were waiting to greet them.

"Hooray, you won!" cried Kendra excitedly. "I couldn't actually tell but Nathan assures me you did."

"Thanks," said Claire. "We got a bit lucky."

The four of them walked to the race office, where the other sailors had gathered. Everyone offered congratulations to Claire and Ryan. Even the Mitchell brothers offered a grudging acknowledgement to them.

"You two deserve a big star for that race," they smirked. Claire looked at them suspiciously, wondering what they meant.

George presented them with a small trophy with a ship's bell mounted on it. "You'll have to leave it here so we can get your names engraved on it. Come and pick it up next week."

Shortly after, the four made their way from the dock to the village. They were all starving so Nathan suggested they go to Beth's Bakery for a cinnamon bun. The smell of warm baking wafted over them through the big screen door. Beth was a short, stout woman in a white apron, who greeted them as they walked in.

"Free cinnamon buns for the race winners!" she said.

Claire blushed. "News travels fast," she said. Soon the four children were picking apart warm gooey cinnamon buns.

"Mmm, this is the best cinnamon bun I've ever had," said Kendra as she licked icing off her fingers.

Finishing the buns, they thanked Beth and went back to the dock. Kendra and Nathan retrieved their bicycles and set off for home, while Claire and Ryan returned to *Pegasus*. As they reached the boat they both stopped short and stared.

Lying in the bottom of the boat was a huge purple starfish.

"Those jerks," said Claire under her breath.

"I guess that's why they said we deserved a star," said Ryan. They looked at each other and both burst out laughing.

"I thought they were being too nice," said Claire. "Well, we showed them at the finish line."

Together they pried the starfish, which was quite hard to unstick, off the bottom of the boat and pitched it overboard. It floated downward before settling on the bottom. They untied *Pegasus* and set off for home.

Back at the house, they retold the events of the

morning to Aunt Jennie and Uncle William. Claire's father chuckled when he heard about the starfish.

"That sounds like something I would have done at your age," he said. "You'll have to think of a suitable revenge."

"Any sign of the whale?" asked Aunt Jennie hurriedly, trying to change the subject. Revenge was something that Claire might take a bit too seriously.

Kendra shook her head sadly. "No sign of it."

"Don't worry, you're bound to see it sooner or later."

After some lunch the four of them sat out on the back patio, eating watermelon and seeing how far they could spit the seeds. Nathan was the best at this game, sending his seeds clear across the lawn and into the flower garden.

"Aunt Jennie will find watermelons growing in her garden next year instead of geraniums," laughed Ryan. Nathan looked a bit worried and everyone laughed.

"What about our treasure hunt?" asked Kendra. "Are we still going to look for the sunken boat?"

"Absolutely," said Claire. "We'll just have to start earlier since it's such a long way out."

"What if we camped on that island?" said Nathan. "The one we landed on during the storm. Then we would be a lot closer to the search area."

"Do you think your parents would let us?" asked

Kendra excitedly. "It would be great to camp on a deserted island!"

"I don't see why not," said Claire. "We have a tent and all the camping gear we need."

"Let's go ask them," said Ryan. He had never been camping without his parents before and he liked the idea of sailing to Whalebone Island and camping there all alone.

They rushed into the house and explained their plan to Aunt Jennie and Uncle William. Uncle William thought it was a splendid idea.

"What will you do about drinking water?" Aunt Jennie asked. "Will you be able to fit everything in *Pegasus*?"

They all looked at each other. It was a tight squeeze even getting the four of them and Meg into *Pegasus*. There was no way it could fit all of them plus the camping gear and food.

"I'm pretty sure there's a small stream on the island," said Nathan. "Although we could take some water with us just in case."

"We can make two trips over there," said Claire. "Someone can stay behind and I'll come back after the first trip to get them and the rest of the supplies. And we can check the water supply on the first trip to see if we need to bring water or not."

Her parents nodded their approval and Nathan

gave a loud cheer.

Next day they began to make preparations. Kendra and Nathan offered to plan the meals. "That's the most important part," Nathan declared.

Claire led Ryan down to the basement where the camping gear was stored. It was all very organized, with stacks of plastic crates lined against the wall, each with a label indicating its contents.

"I guess your mom organized this, not your dad," said Ryan with a grin, thinking of Uncle William's workshop.

"You're right. Thank goodness or we'd never find anything we needed." She began to pull things off the shelves. Tent, sleeping bags, stove, pots. She called out the names as she passed them down to Ryan, who placed them in a pile on the floor. When they were done they took it all upstairs and laid it out on the back patio. When spread out it seemed like an enormous amount of stuff. Claire worried how it would all get into *Pegasus*, even with a second trip. But there was everything they needed, except for a second tent. Claire said they should be able to borrow one from the neighbours and went to call them. She came back shortly.

"We're welcome to borrow it so I'm going to ride over there on my bike to pick it up."

Meanwhile, Aunt Jennie was helping Kendra and

Nathan with the meal planning. They had quickly compiled a list of all their favourite camping foods – hot dogs, marshmallows, mini cereal packages – but had run out of ideas after that.

"You can't live on marshmallows," said Aunt Jennie with a sigh. "And you can have hot dogs for one meal, but not every night. How about a nice vegetable curry?"

Nathan groaned.

"I can make spaghetti," said Kendra. Her aunt agreed that would make a good meal and offered to make a pot of chili as another dinner. For breakfast there would be bacon and eggs, oatmeal, and bagels. Lunch would be sandwiches, with lots of extra snacks in case they got hungry.

"Treasure hunting is hungry work," she said. "The weather is supposed to be very warm, so you'll need to keep things in the cooler and quickly eat up anything that could spoil." They were planning to stay for three nights and things would only stay cool for a day or so, even in the cooler.

Once the full meal list was compiled Aunt Jennie sent them to the pantry to see what they already had. Everything else would have to be picked up from the grocery store that afternoon.

Claire came back with the neighbours' tent and added it to the pile of gear. Nathan and his mother went off to do the grocery shopping while the others packed the camping equipment into bags. Waterproof bags were used for their clothes and sleeping bags to keep them dry during the voyage, and an assortment of canvas duffel bags held the rest of the supplies. To Claire's relief, the amount of gear seemed much smaller when packed into bags.

By evening everything was ready to go, except for a few items in the fridge which would be packed into a cooler the next morning. They went to bed early, anxious for the next day to begin, but it was hard to fall asleep. They all tossed and turned for quite some time until one by one they drifted off.

* * *

Dawn was just breaking when Kendra awoke. A faint light came in through the window, although it was still quite dark. She looked at her watch, which showed 4:45 a.m. on the luminous dial. Kendra sighed softly and glanced over at Claire. Then she sat up with a start; Claire's bed was empty!

Kendra thought for a moment. Where could Claire be? Perhaps that was what had woken her up. After a moment's hesitation, she hopped out of bed and threw on her clothes. Opening the door she peeked into the hallway, but there was no sign of anybody. She tiptoed down the hall, not wanting to wake anyone. Reaching the kitchen, she looked about but there was no sign of Claire. She glanced over to Meg's mat, which also lay empty.

Well, she thought, if Meg's gone then Claire must be outside. She probably woke early and decided to get *Pegasus* ready. Kendra put on her flip flops and went outside. The air was cool and she shivered a bit, wrapping her arms around herself as she made her way down to the dock. Sure enough, there was Claire at the end of the dock next to *Pegasus*. The sail was already up and she was untying the boat as if she were ready to cast off.

Kendra walked to the end of the dock and Meg ran up to her, wagging her tail. Claire looked up and, with an embarrassed smile, mumbled a greeting. In the boat was a large plastic tub, which Kendra recognized from Aunt Jennie's kitchen.

"What are you doing?" she asked.

"Oh, I just thought I'd take *Pegasus* for a quick sail to make sure everything is ship-shape."

"At five in the morning?"

"I couldn't sleep."

There was a pause. Kendra could tell that Claire was hiding something. She looked at the box and Claire followed her gaze. There was a slight fishy smell coming from the boat and Kendra wrinkled her nose.

Claire groaned. "Oh, you may as well know. I'm

going on an expedition of revenge against the Mitchells."

"Really?" said Kendra excitedly. "Can I come?"

"I suppose you'd better, now that you're here. Hop in." Kendra climbed into the boat and Meg followed her, taking up a spot in the bow. Claire cast off and they were soon sailing along in the light morning breeze.

"So what's the plan?" asked Kendra.

"The plan is in that tub. Yesterday I saw seagulls circling on the beach so I went to look and saw there was a dead salmon washed up. I buried it in the sand and covered it with some rocks so the birds wouldn't get it. This morning I retrieved it. We're going to leave it as a surprise in the Mitchells' boat, just like they left the starfish for us."

"Oooh, they won't like that. Do you know where their boat is kept?"

"Their house is about half a kilometre away, in the next bay. They keep their boat anchored off shore since there isn't a dock like ours."

By this time they had almost reached the Mitchells' house. In the centre of the bay was a small sailboat bobbing in the waves. Claire put a finger to her lips and sailed in silently. She brought *Pegasus* into the wind next to the anchored boat and Kendra reached out and grabbed hold of it. Meg looked at them expectantly.

Claire pulled some rubber gloves from her pocket and put them on. She opened the plastic tub and immediately a stench of rotting fish filled the air. She made a face before reaching into the box and pulling out the large fish. Its eyes were missing and chunks of flesh had been picked away by the gulls. Holding it gingerly, Claire put one foot on the side of the boat and prepared to throw the salmon into the Mitchells' boat.

Suddenly a deep voice boomed across the water behind them. "Claire Daniels, what are you doing with that fish?"

~ 11 ~

Off to the Island

The two girls jumped at the sound of the voice. Claire nearly dropped the fish, just managing to hang onto it. Horrified, they slowly turned to look. A short distance away was a small rowboat with a burly looking man with a bushy moustache in it. The two girls had been so engrossed in their work they had failed to hear him rowing up behind them.

Claire and Kendra stood, frozen, with Claire holding the fish out in front of her like a peace offering.

"Uh... Hi Mr. Mitchell," Claire managed to croak.

Mr. Mitchell gave a broad smile. "I hear you won the race yesterday. Congratulations." He paused. "I also heard there was a surprise in your boat. I'm guessing that might have something to do with the fish you're holding?" Claire didn't reply. "I did warn those two you wouldn't be happy about it."

Mr. Mitchell looked toward the shore. "I'd better be getting in now. I need to get my dinner on ice." He bent down and picked up a big beautiful salmon from the floor of his dinghy. "This one looks a lot tastier than yours," he said with a chuckle. He picked up his oars and rowed toward shore with long steady strokes.

Claire and Kendra looked at each other and then

down at the fish in Claire's hands. They both burst out laughing. Stepping across the boat, Claire dropped the fish over the side into the water.

"Now what will we do?" asked Kendra.

Claire shrugged. "I don't know. But we can't go through with it after Mr. Mitchell caught us red-handed."

"We could leave them a black spot," Kendra suggested.

"What's that?"

"It's what pirates leave as a warning to other pirates. A black spot on a piece of paper. It means 'We're going to get you...' "

"All right, let's do that. We can delay our revenge for another time." She pulled a small bag out of one of the hatches and rummaged about in it, eventually coming up with a black felt pen and a sheet of paper. She passed it to Kendra who drew a round circle on the paper and filled it in.

"Where should we put it?"

Claire looked about at the Mitchells' boat. "We'll run it up the mast. Then they'll see it even if they don't come out to the boat." She folded the corner of the paper over and carefully poked a hole through it. She clipped it to a rope and pulled it to the top of the mast, where it fluttered in the wind.

"Do you think they'll know who did it?"

"I'm pretty sure they will," grinned Claire. "And if

they can't figure it out their dad will tell them."

Kendra let go of the Mitchells' boat and *Pegasus* drifted away. Claire turned the boat around and pointed toward home. A short while later they were sneaking down the hallway to their room. Everyone else was still sleeping and in a few minutes Claire and Kendra were asleep again as well.

* * *

A few hours later Claire and Kendra emerged from their room, looking groggy and rubbing their eyes. Ryan and Nathan were eating their breakfast.

"What's with you two?" asked Nathan. "Ryan and I have been up for an hour. We've already taken all the gear down to the dock."

Claire mumbled something unintelligible and shuffled over to the stove where her mother was cooking breakfast. Soon she and Kendra were working their way through a large stack of pancakes and feeling much better.

After finishing breakfast they went down to the dock and put *Pegasus* in the water. The tents, mattresses, and sleeping bags were packed into the boat along with some of the other gear, leaving just enough room for three of them and Meg. Kendra had volunteered to stay behind until Claire returned.

"We'd better bring some snacks," said Nathan, tossing a bag of marshmallows into the boat.

"After that breakfast?" said Claire. "We have our lunch and the marshmallows are for roasting over the campfire." She handed the marshmallows back to Kendra, who placed them with the remaining food.

Aunt Jennie came to see them off. She gave Ryan and Nathan a hug and then she and Kendra waved from the dock as they sailed out of the bay. Kendra watched until the boat disappeared around the point.

The winds were light and it took well over an hour to reach the island. Ryan steered while Claire looked at the chart and Nathan lay in the bow reading. Meg, after circling about for some time trying to find a comfortable spot, lay down on top of the camping gear and went to sleep. They could see Whalebone Island in the distance and watched it grow larger as they drew near. Rounding the corner, they sailed into the cove where they had landed previously and pulled *Pegasus* up on shore.

"Okay, let's get the supplies unloaded," said Claire. "I want to go back for the second load." Ryan and Nathan agreed to scope out a camping site and get the tents set up while she returned for Kendra and the remaining supplies. As soon as the last bag was out of the boat she pushed off and hopped aboard. She turned *Pegasus* around and with a quick wave set off back to Pirate Cove.

Ryan and Nathan looked about them. Meg had wandered toward the blackberry bushes which hid the mouth of the tunnel and was sniffing about. Most of the little cove was flanked by a rocky cliff, but to the right the way was less steep and led to a mossy clearing below the trees. The two boys left the supplies on the beach and clambered up the rocks with Meg following behind. They reached the mossy patch and took a trail leading off into the trees. The trail climbed steeply but soon levelled off. After a short time the trees thinned out and they emerged on the other side of the island.

"Wow, this is perfect!" exclaimed Ryan. It was certainly a magnificent camping spot. In front of them was a rocky bluff overlooking the ocean, with views as far as the eye could see. Not too far away was a tugboat pulling a barge loaded with logs. In the distance they could just make out a ferry crossing the strait. There were a handful of arbutus trees on the bluff, with their strange bare limbs and peeling red bark.

"We can put our tents there," said Nathan, pointing toward a flat spot covered in moss and grass.

Ryan put his hand down and felt the moss. "It feels dry," he said, "and it should be very comfortable to sleep on."

The two boys walked over to the edge of the bluff and looked over. It was a sheer drop to the water below. The water was very dark and they couldn't see the bottom.

"This would be a perfect place for cliff diving," said Nathan. Ryan looked at him as if he'd lost his mind.

"Jump off here?"

"Sure! The water is really deep and it's a clean drop, no risk of hitting any rocks."

"Hmmm, I suppose so," Ryan said without enthusiasm. If there was any cliff diving going on he wanted no part of it. "We'd better go get our stuff and start setting up the tents."

The two boys walked back down the trail to the cove. They gathered as much as they could and began to haul it up to the camp site. It took them several trips. The day was getting warm and both of them were covered in sweat by the time they had finished.

Nathan collapsed at the top as he dropped the last load. "We should have brought a harness for Meg and made her carry some of this stuff," he grumbled. He looked at Meg, who gave a short bark.

"I think she's saying 'Let's go for a swim'," said Ryan. They scrambled down the rocks on the side of the bluff to a flat ledge at the bottom. The tide was high and the water came almost to the edge. Leaving their sandals behind they jumped in with a splash. Meg watched them, pacing back and forth on the ledge and barking, then suddenly jumped in after them. The water was cool and refreshing and they swam in one spot, treading water. After a while they pulled themselves onto the ledge, giving Meg a boost to help her out. They lay on the warm rock, watching the clouds drift overhead.

"When do you think Claire and Kendra will get here?" said Nathan.

Ryan looked at his watch. "I'd say in another hour or so. We'd better get the camp set up before they arrive." But he made no move to get up. Lying in the warm sun with a cool breeze off the water, he felt like he could stay there forever. His home in the city, with the traffic and noise and frantic schedules, seemed a million miles away.

Eventually it was Nathan who got up and put his sandals back on. "Let's get those tents set up," he said and started to scramble back up the rocks. Ryan groaned, but put his shoes on and followed him up the bluff.

At the top they pulled the tents and poles out of their bags and began to assemble them. Nathan insisted he knew which poles went where, but after a while it was clear he did not. It took much trial and error before the two tents were assembled and pegged down in place. They blew up the sleeping mats and put them in the tents, followed by the sleeping bags. Then all the doors and windows were opened to air the tents out.

"Where shall we do our cooking?" said Ryan.

Looking around, they found a natural depression in the rock that would serve as a firepit and put some stones around it to form a fire ring. They chose a flat piece of rock to be the kitchen and brought over the stove and the pots and pans. Spotting an old log, they dragged it over to serve as a bench.

"I'm hungry," said Nathan, and he pulled out the sandwiches Aunt Jennie had made for them. The sun was high overhead now and they were hot again from setting up camp.

"Let's go cliff jumping!" said Nathan, as he finished his sandwich.

Ryan looked at him dubiously. "I think we'd better not."

"Why not?"

"Well, I'm not sure it's safe."

"Sure it is," said Nathan. "You saw how deep the water is."

Ryan felt his stomach tighten. He didn't want to jump off the cliff, which seemed very high to him. On the other hand, he didn't want to admit that to Nathan, who was two years younger and sounded like he jumped off cliffs all the time.

"I'm not sure I can let you do that. Your mother would expect me to be responsible for you."

Nathan looked at him skeptically. "Fine, you go first then," he said, grinning. There was a hint of challenge in his voice.

Ryan looked around hopelessly, as if some distraction might suddenly appear to get him out of this fix. Sighing to himself, he walked to the cliff edge and looked over. The tide had gone down a bit so the drop was even higher than before. He kicked off his sandals and inched his way to the edge. He could feel his legs shaking and hoped that Nathan couldn't tell. He knew he couldn't turn back now, although Nathan hadn't said a word since he'd walked out to the ledge.

He took a deep breath and stepped out from the rock. The surface of the water hurtled toward him and his feet hit the surface. Suddenly he was underwater. It seemed to take ages before he stopped sinking and started to float back up. Then his head popped out and he took a great gulp of air. A wave of relief swept over him as he realized that he'd done it! There was a loud cheer and he looked up to see *Pegasus* a short distance away, with Claire and Kendra waving madly at him. From above Nathan was looking down at him and hooting loudly. Meg was barking furiously. Ryan swam slowly to the ledge where they had swum earlier and sat with his legs dangling in the water, breathing heavily. He felt drained, yet immensely exhilarated.

Claire and Kendra sailed in and stopped a few feet away. "What are you doing?" demanded Claire, half laughing, half serious. "Are you crazy?"

Ryan took a deep breath.

Ryan shrugged. "Nathan wanted to do it and I felt I should go first to make sure it was safe." He looked up at Nathan, who was still on top of the bluff. "Aren't you going to jump?" he called to him.

"He's certainly not!" said Claire. "It's far too high!"

Ryan looked surprised. "I thought you two jumped off cliffs like this all the time?"

"Not anything this high! This is at least twice as high as any cliff we've jumped off before."

Ryan turned to Nathan, who looked at him guiltily. "I didn't quite realize how high it was until you were about to jump," he said.

Ryan groaned and lay back on the ledge.

"Well, I thought it was great," said Kendra. "Way to go!" She couldn't believe that Ryan had jumped from such a height. He was usually the last person to try something like that.

"It was pretty impressive," admitted Claire. "Now come down to the cove and help us with the rest of the gear. We'll meet you there." She turned *Pegasus* around and they set off for the other side of the island.

Ryan climbed back to the top of the bluff and he and Nathan walked back down the path to the cove. Meg stuck close to him, rubbing up against his legs and almost tripping him. She'd been very surprised to see Ryan go over the edge and wanted to make sure he didn't disappear like that again!

~ 12 ~

This Means War!

They met *Pegasus* on the other side and together carried the remaining gear up to the campsite. Claire and Kendra were impressed with the camping spot.

"We'll be able to look out and see the sea when we wake up," said Kendra. The tents were arranged side by side facing the ocean.

"It's pretty exposed," said Claire. "But the weather forecast is good so that shouldn't be a problem."

They put the cooler in the shade and hung the remaining food in a tree so animals wouldn't get into it. Since it was already past two o'clock they decided to leave the treasure hunting until tomorrow and spend the day swimming and exploring the island. The girls had already eaten their lunch while in the boat and were ready to cool off, so they went back down to the rock ledge for a swim. Afterwards they lazed in the sun.

A number of sailboats were out that day and Claire pulled out her binoculars to see if she could identify any of them. Suddenly she sat up and focused on a small boat that was headed in their direction.

"What's up?" asked Ryan, noticing her intent look.

"I think it's those rotten Mitchell boys again," she replied. "And they seem to be coming this way."

"Why would they be coming here?"

Claire and Kendra glanced at each other. Then they admitted the whole story of their revenge expedition to the Mitchells' place. Nathan roared with laughter.

"I thought I smelled fish this morning when we got into *Pegasus*. That's why you two looked so tired. I bet Mr. Mitchell is telling Dad about it right now; they see each other all the time."

"So why do you think they're coming here?" asked Ryan.

"I don't know. Maybe they want to challenge us over the black spot. Or maybe they're just out for a sail. Who knows?"

The four of them watched in silence as the boat drew nearer. Soon it was close enough to see the two boys clearly. The boat changed direction slightly and came toward them. When it was only a few metres away it turned and drifted slowly in front of the rock ledge.

"What are you doing here?" demanded Claire.

"We're here because of your black spot," Matthew Mitchell sneered. "We're not afraid of that. In fact, we're here to give it back to you." His brother Flint reached down into the boat and picked up a paper airplane, made from the sheet of paper that Kendra had drawn the black spot on. It arced neatly through the air and landed at Claire's feet. Meg ran up and pounced on it, picking it up in her mouth and shaking it back and forth.

Suddenly, at some unseen signal, the two boys reached into the boat and pulled out an enormous water gun. They began to fire sheets of a sticky red liquid at the four children who, shrieking, scrambled to get out of the way. But there was nowhere to hide on the little rock ledge. They tripped over one another as Meg, barking furiously, ran between their legs. At last they managed to clamber up the rocks to safety, but not before they were all covered in the sticky liquid.

They looked down from the bluff at the Mitchell brothers, who were hooting with laughter as they sailed away.

"Ugh, what a mess!" said Nathan. "What is this stuff?"

Kendra looked ruefully at her new swimsuit, which was covered in red stains. "I think it's some kind of soda pop mixed with water."

"Mmm, it tastes quite good," said Nathan, licking his fingers.

Claire looked furious. "This means war," she said grimly.

They went back down to the rock ledge and dove into the ocean to rinse themselves off. Meg had to be thrown in the water as she refused to go in on her own, preferring to lick the sticky liquid off her fur. Gathering up their things, they went back up the bluff.

To the south they could still see the Mitchells' boat. But instead of sailing back toward their home it was rounding the tip of the island.

"What are they doing?" Claire muttered.

"The cove!" cried Ryan. "They're going to attack *Pegasus*!"

At once they rushed down the path to the cove. As they got there the Mitchells' boat was just passing through the narrow entrance. Together they pushed *Pegasus* into the water. Seeing them come, Matthew Mitchell turned the boat around while Flint fired a few more shots of the sticky red liquid at *Pegasus*.

"Quick, they're getting away!" said Claire. She climbed in and pulled the sail up as quickly as possible. Before anyone could stop her, Meg jumped in and scampered to the front of the boat.

"Where's Kendra?" asked Nathan.

He looked around and saw Kendra scrambling over the rocks to a point near the entrance. She arrived just as the Mitchells passed by and flung herself into the water, reaching the side of their boat with a few powerful strokes. She grabbed hold of the bow line which was dangling over the side and pulled on it, causing their boat to swerve sideways and come to a halt. The boom swung across and the boys ducked just in time to avoid being hit. Kendra felt herself being dragged behind the boat, water splashing in her eyes and nose as she tried desperately to hang on. Flint was jerking on the line, trying to pull it out of her hands. At last she couldn't hold on any longer and let go, watching the boat lurch away from her.

"Kendra!" cried a voice. Kendra looked around to see *Pegasus* coming up behind her. Ryan and Nathan reached over and grabbed her arms, pulling her over the side. She sat in the bottom of the boat, trying to catch her breath.

"Great work!" said Claire. "You slowed them down. Now we have a chance to catch them!"

They were only a short distance behind the other boat. The Mitchells had chosen to go downwind and Claire carefully picked a position behind them that blocked the wind with their sail.

"What are we going to do when we catch them?" asked Kendra.

"I'm not sure," admitted Claire.

"Board them and take them prisoner!" declared Nathan in a bloodthirsty pirate voice. Ryan looked at him dubiously.

Slowly but surely they closed the gap until they were only a few metres away. Flint tried to fire the water gun at them, but it was all out of the red liquid.

He leaned over the side to fill it with water, but that slowed them even more.

Claire steered *Pegasus* behind the Mitchells' boat. Meg was standing on the bow, intently watching the other boat and wagging her tail furiously. She thought this was all great fun! She recognized the Mitchell boys and wondered if they would have more of that delicious sticky red liquid for her!

"Surrender or we'll sink your ship!" cried Nathan.

"Never!" yelled Matthew as he turned the boat directly into the path of *Pegasus*. Claire tried to turn away but it was too late and the two boats collided with a sickening bang.

The sudden jolt caused Meg to lose her balance. To save herself from falling in the water she jumped onto the Mitchells' boat. But the deck of their boat was also covered in the red liquid, and as she landed her paws shot out from underneath her. Legs flailing, she slid heavily across the deck right into Matthew's lap!

The boy was so surprised that he let go of the tiller and fell over backwards. With no one steering, their boat swung wildly around and tilted over sharply, dumping both boys into the sea. They came up spluttering.

With only Meg on board, the boat sailed off a little way before turning into the wind and coming to a halt. Meg stood in the cockpit, looking surprised and wondering what had just happened. Claire quickly sailed over and Nathan hopped into the boat with Meg. Flint gave a shout and started swimming toward him as fast as he could, but Nathan pulled in the sail and began to move away. He soon gave up the chase and shouted angrily at him to bring back their boat.

The others rendezvoused with Nathan and pulled the two boats into the wind together.

"You did it, Meg! You've captured their boat!" said Kendra. Meg wagged her tail and began to lick up the red liquid on the deck.

"What will we do now that we've got it?" asked Claire.

"Let's sink it!" said Nathan.

"We can't do that. Besides, it's a nice boat and it would be a shame to sink it."

"Then let's just keep it. We could do with a second boat now there are four of us."

"C'mon, we can't do that either. They'd tell the police we'd stolen it and we'd be in all kinds of trouble. And they have to get back home somehow," she added.

"What about towing it home as captured booty with them as our prisoners for ransom?" said Ryan. "We could take the sail and paddles out and tow them home. They won't be able to escape because we'll have their sail."

Everyone agreed that sounded like a good plan.

Nathan dropped the sail and passed it to Kendra, along with the paddles. He found a long rope in one of the hatches and tied the two boats together, then clambered back on board *Pegasus*.

"Wait!" said Claire. She dug about and pulled out a blue flag with a winged horse, identical to the one flying from *Pegasus'* mast. "They can travel under our flag."

Nathan ran the flag up the mast, where it fluttered in the breeze. They sailed back to where the Mitchells were still treading water.

"All right, you win!" they cried. "Now give us our boat back! We're getting cold and tired here."

"We're taking you home as our prisoners!" called Claire. She circled around so their boat swung near and they clambered over the side. The line between the two boats pulled taut and they set sail for the bay where the Mitchells lived, towing their prisoners behind them.

It was slow going pulling the other boat and nearly six o'clock by the time the Mitchells' dock came into view. As they entered the bay Claire untied the tow rope and left the Mitchells adrift, sailing on toward the dock. Mr. and Ms. Mitchell were sitting with some friends at the end of the dock, enjoying the late afternoon sun.

"Ahoy, there!" called Mr. Mitchell, who had been

watching them through binoculars. "I see you have some prisoners."

"Yes, and we've come to ransom them back!" said Kendra with a mischievous grin.

"What if we don't want them back?" he laughed.

"We'll send them to the bottom!" said Nathan, doing another pirate imitation.

"Well, in that case, we'd better pay up," said Mrs. Mitchell. "How about a lemon loaf as payment? I just baked two and you could have one."

"Oooh, yes. I love lemon loaf!" said Nathan and the others agreed it would make a fine ransom.

Mrs. Mitchell disappeared into the house and came back a few minutes later with a lemon loaf wrapped in a bag. "Here you go," she said.

The children thanked her and Ryan handed over the boy's sail.

"We'll give them their paddle as we go by," said Claire. "But they have to promise to return our flag."

The Mitchells assured them the flag would be returned and gave them a push out from the dock. They sailed past their prisoners and passed them their paddle. Flint took it back with a scowl. "This isn't the end of this, you know," he said.

Claire shrugged, and with a farewell wave, set off for Whalebone Island.

~ 13 ~

The Search Continues

By the time they got back the sun was low in the sky. Claire brought *Pegasus* into the cove and up on the beach. They gathered some driftwood and carried it back to the camp in order to make a fire that evening.

"We'd better make dinner quickly while there's still light," said Claire when they reached the camp. She went to the cooler to pull out the chili Aunt Jennie had prepared for them, but it was still frozen solid.

"I'll make spaghetti instead," said Kendra.

She set to work preparing the sauce on the propane stove, while Nathan fetched a pot of water from the sea. "You won't need to salt it," he laughed.

While Kendra made dinner, Claire and Ryan lit the fire. There was no paper so they had to start it with bits of dry grass and twigs, but soon it was crackling away. Dinner was ready just as the sun was setting, and they sat on the log and ate their spaghetti while the sun bathed the mountains in a warm pink glow.

After dinner they washed the dishes and roasted marshmallows over the fire, talking and laughing about their battle with the Mitchells.

Nathan was the first to yawn, which set them all

to yawning, even Meg. It was such a beautiful evening that nobody wanted to go to bed, but Claire insisted they get a good night's sleep. "We've got a big day of treasure hunting tomorrow," she said.

They crawled into their tents, Claire and Kendra in one and Ryan and Nathan in the other. Meg was left outside but after a few minutes of listening to her whine Nathan unzipped the door and let her into the tent. She circled a few times and then curled up at the foot of his sleeping bag. Within a few minutes all of them were asleep.

* * *

The next morning they were awakened early by the sun streaming into the tent. Ryan was up first, followed by Claire and Kendra. Only Nathan continued to sleep, oblivious to the sun.

"So much for lying in bed watching the view," said Ryan. "It's way too hot in the tent."

He set about preparing bacon and eggs for breakfast. The bacon needed to be eaten up the first day while the cooler was still cold. After that it would be oatmeal and bagels for breakfast. Nathan stumbled out of the tent after a while, rubbing his eyes. "The smell of bacon woke me up," he said.

After breakfast they tidied up the camp and hung the food in a tree so it would be safe from any animals that might be about. They packed a lunch and launched *Pegasus*, setting off for the area they had spotted on the chart a few days before. It wasn't too far away from the island and they soon reached the place where the shallows were supposed to be. Kendra peered over the side of the boat but the water looked dark and deep.

Suddenly the sea brightened and they were over the sandbar. The water was eight or ten metres deep at this point and they could just see the sandy bottom below. Claire checked her chart.

"It's still too deep here, a boat could never have hit bottom. We need to go further east where the sand bar is shallower."

She turned the boat in a new direction. The sand bar was quite large, running almost two kilometres from east to west and about 400 metres wide. As they sailed east the water got shallower and shallower. There were various objects on the bottom – an old tire, sunken logs, and something that appeared to be the axle of a car. But no sign of anything that might be part of a sunken boat.

At length they reached the shallowest part of the sandbar. The water was very clear here and sand dollars were strewn across the bottom. Small fish swam beneath them, casting small shadows. Here and there big boulders protruded from the sand.

"If they hit one of those it would do some damage,"

said Ryan, pointing at a large boulder embedded in the sand and covered in barnacles. "But it still seems too deep to hit, even in a storm."

"We're not at low tide yet," replied Claire. "In another two hours the sea level will probably drop another metre. That still won't be as low as it was the night the boat sank, though."

"We won't need to snorkel this time," said Kendra. "We can just look from the boat."

Claire sailed to a point at the far end of the shallow area and then turned around. They began to make long passes back and forth, everyone craning their necks over the side and peering into the water. It was difficult to see on the south side of the boat as the reflection off the water dazzled them. But on the north side they could easily see through the shadow cast by *Pegasus*.

Meg also peered over the side, wondering what everyone was looking for so intently. Whenever she saw a fish she gave a little bark to let them know but no one paid her any attention. After a while she gave up and settled in the bottom of the boat for a nap.

Back and forth they went without success. Once Nathan cried out that he had seen something but it turned out to be an old piece of dock. The day was getting hot so they dropped the anchor and went for a swim.

Once back on board and drying off, they all admitted to being a bit disheartened.

"Let's just go back to the island and go swimming," said Nathan, who had clearly grown bored with the search.

"If it was ever here, it probably drifted off the sandbar into deep water," said Ryan.

Claire nodded. "It does seem pretty unlikely we're going to find it," she said resignedly.

Only Kendra still seemed willing to continue on. "We should at least finish searching this area," she said. "There's not much more to cover and then we'll know for certain it's not here."

The others reluctantly agreed and they went back to sweeping the area. Ryan took over the helm from Claire who watched over the side in his place. Nathan had given up completely and was reading a book. The water got deeper to the north until at last, they could see the edge of the sandbar, where the colour of the water changed as the depth increased.

"This will be the last sweep," said Claire and Kendra nodded.

As they were reaching the end of the run, Kendra suddenly spied something dark on the bottom ahead.

"What's that?" she said, clutching Claire's arm. Claire came to her side of the boat and peered down as they drew closer. There was definitely something there but Claire was sure it would be another false alarm. Ryan slowed *Pegasus* as they came near.

"Look!" shrieked Kendra. "It's a boat!"

~ 14 ~

A Mysterious Boat

They all peered over the edge where Kendra was pointing. On the sea bottom, the remains of an old boat could clearly be seen. It was a wooden motorboat, perhaps six or seven metres long, resting on its side and half buried in the sand. Most of what they could see was the round curve of the hull. The bottom was covered in algae and encrusted with barnacles and mussels.

The children could hardly contain their excitement. They took down the sail and paddled over the site of the wreck.

"Do you really think that's it?" asked Claire.

"It's in the right place," said Ryan. "And it's a motorboat about the right size. It must be the one we're looking for!"

"I don't see a hole in the hull where it hit the rocks," said Nathan.

"It could be on the other side, the side that's buried in the sand," said Kendra. She was convinced this was the *Gypsy Moth*. And if not, it hardly mattered; they had found a sunken wreck!

"All right, since you saw it first, you should be first to dive down and take a look at it," Claire said to Kendra.

Ryan dropped the anchor over the side, keeping them far enough away from the wreck that it wouldn't interfere with the diving. Kendra put on her mask, snorkel and fins and rolled over the side of the boat with a splash.

"Be careful," warned Claire. "Don't go inside the hull." Kendra nodded and put her head down. She swam slowly over the wreck, her feet moving languidly under the water. She circled a few times, occasionally blowing water out the top of her snorkel. Then she arched her back and dove toward the bottom. The others could see her reach the boat and swim alongside it before coming back up for air. She burst through the surface and pulled the snorkel out of her mouth.

"This is it!" she called. "I can see the name on the side – it's the *Gypsy Moth*!"

"What else could you see?" the others asked eagerly.

"Not too much. It's quite deep and I couldn't stay down too long. But I could see a few things inside. I'm going down again." She turned and began another dive to the sunken boat.

"I want to go too!" said Nathan. Soon they were all in the water with their masks and fins, diving down to look at the wreck. As Kendra had said, it was deeper than it looked and they could only stay down a short time before returning to the surface. After each dive

She arched her back and dove toward the wreck.

they would tread water to catch their breath, relating excitedly to each other what they'd seen.

The boat had an open cockpit with a small storage area in the bow. It had an inboard engine and a propeller could be seen sticking out the back transom, with the words *Gypsy Moth* stencilled above it. Near the bow on the side facing the sand was the beginning of a large jagged tear in the hull, which was obviously where the boat had hit the rock that caused it to sink.

Inside the cockpit were a few personal effects lying against a broken window. A cell phone, a rusty pocket knife, a broken coffee mug. The keys were still in the ignition. Claire reached to pull out a map from a side pocket but it fell apart in her hands. She tried to open the storage hatch but it was locked. Kendra spotted something pink under one of the seats, which turned out to be a stuffed pink rabbit.

After twenty minutes or so they clambered back onto *Pegasus*. They were all shivering from the water, which was much colder down at the bottom than it was near the surface. They laid the things they had found out on the deck to dry.

"Not exactly treasure," said Nathan through chattering teeth. He tried to turn on the cell phone but it wouldn't work.

Ryan laughed. "I don't think you'll get that to work after three years in salt water."

"I suppose not," said Nathan. He shook it and water flew out.

"At least we found the boat," said Claire. "The police will be happy to know where it is."

"I'm sure this is a treasure for someone," said Kendra, holding up the pink rabbit. "We can return it to the owners."

Once the sun had dried them off and warmed them up, they put the sail back up and raised the anchor to return to Whalebone Island. Before they left, they carefully noted their location on Claire's chart so they could find the wreck another time. On the way back to their camp they chattered excitedly about the wreck until they could talk no more, then lapsed into silence. The exertion of diving so many times had tired them all out. By the time they reached the little cove Nathan and Kendra both had their eyes closed, and Claire was trying to stifle her yawns.

"An early dinner tonight I think," said Claire, trudging up the path to the campsite. Kendra cooked up the chili, which was now thawed, and served it with a squished loaf of bread they had brought. They were all ravenous and the pot was empty in no time.

"I'm still hungry," said Nathan.

"Why don't we have some blackberries?" suggested Claire. "There are lots around."

They all went off to look for blackberries. Besides

the ones in the cove, there was another large patch near their campsite. Claire and Kendra soon had their fill but Ryan and Nathan continued to gorge themselves. When he returned to camp Ryan was holding his stomach and groaning.

"Uh oh, I think I might have eaten too many blackberries," he said.

"Mom's going to have a fit when she sees that shirt," said Claire, looking at Nathan's t-shirt. It was covered in deep purple blackberry stains. He shrugged.

"Marshmallows?" he asked hopefully.

"Not a chance, you glutton! You'll be ill if you have marshmallows on top of all those blackberries."

"I can't believe you could eat marshmallows after all that," said Ryan, who looked rather queasy. "I just want to lie down." He said goodnight and went to his tent.

The sun was setting and they were all very tired, so Claire, Kendra, and Nathan weren't long in following Ryan to bed. They were soon asleep, except for Ryan, who lay in his sleeping bag holding his stomach. He felt very bloated and wished he hadn't eaten so much. At last he too fell asleep, but it was a restless slumber and he dreamt that when he opened the hatch of the sunken boat it was filled with blackberries.

* * *

When Ryan awoke it was still pitch black in the tent. His stomach felt somewhat better but it was very hot and he was sweating in his sleeping bag. He looked at his watch – half past two. He unzipped his sleeping bag to cool off and tried to go back to sleep. For a while he tossed and turned, trying to get comfortable. But he felt hot and sticky and now his stomach was starting to rumble again. Finally he sat up, opened the tent door and crawled out.

Outside it was unusually warm. The clouds above were just beginning to break up, allowing a little bit of light from the moon, but it was still very dark. Ryan stepped carefully through the camp, not wanting to wake anyone. He walked out to the bluff, where he stood and gazed across at the distant lights on the mainland. He had been hoping for a breeze to cool him off, but the night was absolutely still. He contemplated going for a swim.

While he stood there he noticed a faint humming sound, which gradually got louder. Must be a boat engine, he thought, but it's a strange time to be out on the water. He wondered if it was a tugboat or barge, taking advantage of the tides. It sounded quite close now and he peered into the darkness but could see nothing.

Suddenly the clouds parted and the moonlight shone through. Ryan was startled to see the outline of a large fishing boat almost directly in front of him. It had no lights on and was moving very slowly, its motor making the low humming noise he had been listening to. Ryan watched in amazement.

That's very strange, he thought. And dangerous too, out on a dark night with no lights. He watched the boat motor down to the end of the island and disappear around the point. A minute or so later he heard what sounded like an anchor chain being let out and shortly after the motor shut off.

Ryan's curiosity was piqued. The boat was far too large to anchor in the little cove, he thought, yet there was no safe anchorage outside it. He decided to go investigate. He went into the forest and down the trail to the other side of the island. It was very dark in the woods and he didn't have his flashlight, so he had to go slowly to avoid stumbling over roots in the path. But he had made the trip so many times now that he knew the way quite well and he soon emerged at the mossy opening above the beach.

The moon was brighter now and he could see the boat quite clearly in front of him. There were two men on board and a third was climbing down a ladder to a dinghy below. Once he reached the dinghy, one of the other men climbed down after him. The second man sat in the bow of the dinghy while the first rowed them into the cove. Ryan crouched down to be sure they wouldn't see him.

The men landed the dinghy and Ryan saw one of them point at *Pegasus* pulled up on the beach. They spoke to each other in low tones but he couldn't hear what was said. Then they made their way to the back of the blackberry bush where the mouth of the tunnel lay. They were gone for some time, but eventually returned carrying something between them. The moon had gone behind a cloud momentarily and Ryan couldn't make out what was being carried, other than it seemed bulky and awkward. They placed it carefully in the dinghy and rowed back to the fishing boat. The man who had remained helped them bring the object on board. Ryan heard the engines start and the clank of the anchor chain being pulled up. The fishing boat slowly motored off into the night, leaving a silvery wake behind them.

Ryan watched until it disappeared into the dark. He wanted to go down to the tunnel and investigate but he knew it would be foolhardy to try and climb down in the dark. It would have to wait until morning. He made his way back to their camp and crawled back into the tent, taking care not to wake Nathan. Meg opened one eye and looked at him, then closed it again. Ryan lay down on his sleeping bag and tried to fall back asleep. But he couldn't stop thinking about the mysterious boat and the men he'd seen. What were they up to?

~ 15 ~

Exploring the Island

At breakfast the next morning, Ryan told the others what he had seen in the night.

"That's very strange," said Claire. "What could they be doing? It sounds like they're storing something on the island, but why would they come at night?"

"And why would they keep their lights off?" added Kendra.

"Let's go look in the tunnel!" said Nathan.

"As soon as we've cleaned up and done the dishes," said Claire. "Then we can check it out."

Soon they were making their way down the path to the cove. Scrambling over the rocks to the beach, they pushed their way through the blackberry bushes to the tunnel entrance behind. This time they had brought their flashlights and they shone them around the tunnel walls. They came to the place where the tunnel was blocked by the door and looked around.

"There's no sign of anything," said Nathan. "Are you sure you didn't dream this last night?"

Ryan glared at him. "Of course not. I'd know if I had dreamt it."

"I didn't hear you get up," said Nathan.

"That doesn't mean anything. You'd sleep through

an earthquake!" said Claire. "Perhaps they took away whatever was stored here."

"Maybe they have a key to the lock and are keeping things inside," said Kendra.

"That seems more likely," said Ryan. "If they're using this as a hiding place, they may have put their own lock on. This lock looks new."

He shone his light on the lock and peered at it. It was a shiny new lock, not in keeping with the old wooden door. The latch was also new and very sturdy looking. Nathan gave it a shake but it was securely locked.

"Well, I guess there's nothing more we can do," said Ryan, his voice tinged with disappointment. "But I really did see them."

They made their way out of the tunnel and back up to the camp. With their search for the sunken boat complete, the day was free to do as they pleased.

Kendra and Nathan collected a huge pile of driftwood from the beach so there would be plenty of firewood that evening. Then Ryan and Kendra took *Pegasus* out for a sail, while Claire and Nathan stayed behind. It was the first time they had been sailing on their own. Claire gave them a few last tips before they left and pointed out some spots on the chart to avoid.

"If the wind starts to pick up, come straight back," she said. "You don't want to be caught out in a storm like the one we were in before."

They promised they would and set off from the cove, Ryan steering and Kendra controlling the sail. It felt liberating to be out in the little boat on their own, with only the wind to take them wherever they wanted to go. Ryan looked at Kendra and she laughed.

"I don't think I've ever seen such a big smile on your face," she teased him. Ryan just grinned more broadly. They went past the tip of Whalebone Island and continued up the coast until they came to a small bay with an old dock and an abandoned house, its roof almost covered in blackberry vines. Then Ryan turned around and sailed back down the other side of the island. Up on the bluff they could see their tents and Claire and Nathan reading their books. Claire picked up the binoculars to look at them and Kendra waved to her. Nathan glanced at them and waved briefly, then went back to his book.

After circling the island they returned to the cove. Claire was there to meet them.

"How did it go?"

"It was great!" said Ryan enthusiastically. "We went as far as a little bay with an old abandoned house."

"That's the old Davidson farm," said Claire. "They were early homesteaders here and lived there until they died. But it's been abandoned for years now."

She helped them pull *Pegasus* on shore and they

walked back to the camp. Nathan was busy making lunch and handed sandwiches to them as they returned. They ate their lunch and afterwards had a lazy afternoon swimming, reading, and lying in the sun on the warm rocks.

Toward the end of the afternoon, Kendra and Nathan decided to draw a map of the island. Getting out some paper and pencils they had brought, Kendra drew an outline of the island based on the tiny one shown on Claire's chart. She marked all the places they knew – the cove where *Pegasus* was pulled up, the tunnel entrance, the camp site, and the swimming ledge.

"Let's mark all the blackberry bushes," said Nathan, marking them on the map with a carefully drawn blackberry.

"What else?" asked Kendra.

"We could do some more exploring and see what else there is," suggested Nathan. Together the two began to investigate the rest of the island. It was not a large island, perhaps 500 metres long and 200 metres wide. First they climbed to the highest point where there was a rocky lookout facing south. Then they made their way to the north tip. At the very end, there was a rock bluff that dropped straight into the sea, similar to the one near their campsite but not nearly as high.

"This would be better for cliff jumping," said Nathan. "Seriously, it's much lower than where Ryan jumped", he added, seeing Kendra's dubious look. He marked it on the map, although Kendra insisted on adding a question mark.

They continued around the other side of the island, back toward the cove, and came upon a small bluff with a mossy patch below it.

"We'll have to go around," said Kendra and she started to double back.

"Why? We can jump down this," said Nathan. "Watch!"

Kendra turned and looked as he went to the edge of the small bluff, crouched down, and jumped off. As he landed on the ground below there was a sickening sound of cracking wood. In horror, Kendra watched as Nathan disappeared from sight through the moss!

Nathan disappeared from sight through the moss.

~ 16 ~

Nathan's Discovery

Nathan was so surprised when he fell through the hole he didn't even cry out. Almost immediately his feet landed on a hard surface, but it was steeply sloped. His feet shot out from under him and he came down hard on the seat of his pants. Then he continued to slide. He put his hands out and felt for something to grab on to, but the surface was smooth rock. Suddenly he felt himself falling through the air for a second time and a moment later he landed with a thud.

He lay on the ground for a while, gasping for air. The hard fall had knocked the wind out of him. He felt bruised and battered but otherwise okay. He looked around but it was pitch black. All he could see was a faint glimmer of light from above, which he assumed must be the hole he had fallen down.

He faintly heard Kendra calling him from above. Then a bit more light came in from above and he heard her voice more clearly. "Nathan, are you all right?"

"Yes, I'm fine," he answered, although he didn't really feel fine.

"Where are you?"

"I'm in some sort of cave! Although it's too dark to see much." He could hear Kendra pulling at something and a shower of dirt fell on him from above.

"Hey, be careful!" he called up.

"Sorry! I'm just trying to open up this hole a bit more so I can see you. It looks like it was covered with a wooden lid but the wood has rotted and it broke when you landed on it." There was a pause and a scraping noise as more dirt fell down on him. Soon the opening became brighter. To his relief he saw Kendra's face looking down at him. She smiled and waved.

"Wow, that's a long way down. Did you break anything?"

"No, I don't think so." Nathan had gotten to his feet by now and although he was very sore, nothing seemed to be broken. He looked up toward Kendra. Above him, a round, smooth shaft angled steeply upwards. "I think I'm in the mine tunnel! I must have fallen down an old ventilation shaft!"

"Well, I'm glad you're not hurt. You gave me quite a scare!"

"I gave myself quite a scare! You'd better go back and tell Claire and Ryan. I don't know how I'm going to get out of here."

"Okay, don't go anywhere!" Kendra ran back to the camp to get help while Nathan waited in the tunnel, peering into the gloom. Although there was a bit more light now that Kendra had uncovered the shaft, he still couldn't see more than a few feet around him. Beyond that it was pitch black and absolutely silent.

"Nathan?" He heard Claire's voice and saw her looking down the shaft.

"Hi," he said, giving her a wave.

"What are you doing down there?"

"Having a party," he replied sarcastically. "What do you think I'm doing?"

"Sorry." Claire paused. "Are you okay?"

"If you mean have I broken anything, the answer's no. But I have no idea how I'm going to get out. The shaft opening is too high; I can't even reach it."

Claire's head disappeared and he heard the three of them talking among themselves, but he couldn't make out what they were saying. Then she reappeared.

"We're going to get a rope to pull you out. We'll get the anchor rope from *Pegasus.*"

"Good idea. Can you bring me a flashlight too? I'd like to take a look around before you pull me back up."

She disappeared and Ryan's head appeared in her place. "Gee, you're lucky you didn't break anything. That's a long way down. I'm not sure the rope is going to reach."

Nathan felt his heart sink. He had also been thinking the rope might not be long enough but he didn't want to admit that possibility to himself. He heard Kendra say something and Ryan hurriedly added, "Oh, it probably will. That anchor rope is pretty long."

Claire came back with the rope and a flashlight. She wrapped the flashlight in a small towel and put it in a bag. "Look out!" she called and dropped it down the shaft.

Nathan stepped back as he heard the bag tumbling down the shaft. It dropped onto the ground in front of him. He pulled out the flashlight and switched it on. Now he could see clearly that he was indeed in the old mine tunnel, but on the other side of the locked door. He went over to the door and shook it but of course, it would not open. He shone the flashlight around and then stopped. Stacked up on one side were a number of large rectangular objects, wrapped in plastic.

These must be what Ryan saw the men carrying, he thought to himself. He went closer and shone his light on them. There were a variety of sizes, ranging from the size of a large book to one as big as a double bed! Each had a number written on its plastic wrapper. He lifted one up and was surprised to find it wasn't very heavy.

Nathan peeled back the plastic to reveal a cardboard box underneath. He opened the end of the box and inside he could see something covered in bubble wrap. He slid it gently out of the box and carefully pulled away the bubble wrap.

He found himself looking at a painting in a heavy wood frame. It was a dark forest scene with huge trees, done in thick swirling greens and blues. It was unlike any painting Nathan had seen before and even in the dim light he was amazed at how beautiful it looked.

He heard Claire's voice calling and he ran back to the ventilation shaft. "Hey, guess what I've found!" he shouted. His voice echoed crazily around the tunnel. Claire poked her head down.

"We're just about ready to pull you up," she said.

"No, wait! I've found the stolen art!" he cried.

"What are you talking about?" she said.

"The stolen art that Sergeant Sandhu told us about!" he said. "It's all here in the mine tunnel! The thieves must be storing it here until they find buyers for the paintings. Ryan must have seen them taking one away to be sold."

Kendra and Ryan were peering over Claire's shoulder now.

"See, I didn't dream it," said Ryan.

"So that's what they were doing," said Claire thoughtfully. "That explains why they would be coming here in the middle of the night with no lights."

"We'd better let Sergeant Sandhu know as soon as possible," said Kendra.

"Yes," said Claire. "But first we have to get Nathan out."

Nathan went back and carefully returned the painting to its box and replaced the plastic wrapping. Meanwhile, Claire was lowering a rope with a loop at the end. It caught on the rock every so often and she had to give it a shake to keep it going. Finally, it stopped near the end of the shaft.

"A bit further!" he called.

"It won't go any further," said Claire. "Can you reach it?"

Nathan tried to jump and grab the rope but it was still well out of his reach.

"No! Can't you let it down any further?"

"That's as far as it will go."

"Isn't there any other rope?"

"Nothing that would hold your weight," said Claire. There was silence at both ends of the rope as the situation sank in.

Finally, Claire spoke. "I'll just have to go and get help," she said. "It won't take too long and you're perfectly safe here. I'll be back in a couple of hours, well before dark."

"Okay," said Nathan, but his voice was quiet and strained. He didn't like the idea of being stuck in the tunnel for a long time. "Will anyone stay here with me?"

"Of course. Kendra and Ryan will stay here while I go."

This made Nathan feel somewhat better. He supposed it wouldn't be too bad as long as Ryan and Kendra were up above and Claire was back before dark. "Can you throw me down a sweater?" he said. "It's getting a bit cold down here."

"Sure. I'm going to get started." Claire turned to Kendra and Ryan. "He wants a sweater. Stay close to him. He'll probably want some food soon – he's usually hungry. I should be back in a few hours." With that she hurried down the slope toward the cove.

A short while later she was making good progress toward home, with a nice wind at her back. She could see Pirate Cove and expected to be there within the hour. Suddenly, without warning, a gust of wind pushed the sail over. Claire pulled hard on the tiller to correct her course and there was a loud crack. She felt herself falling backward and landed with a splash in the water. Holding the broken end of the tiller in her hand, she watched as *Pegasus* sailed away from her!

~ 17 ~

Hostage!

Kendra and Ryan sat at the top of the shaft, chatting with Nathan to keep him company. Ryan brought him a fleece jacket and some jeans to keep warm, as well as some water to drink. As Claire had expected, he was soon complaining he was hungry, so Kendra went back to camp and cooked up some hot dogs. She wrapped two up in aluminum foil and dropped them down the hole. Soon after he asked for a book to read. They sent it down to him along with some spare batteries for his flashlight. Nathan found a spot that wasn't too uncomfortable and settled down to read.

The sun dropped lower in the sky and Ryan and Kendra found themselves checking their watches more and more frequently. Claire had been gone for nearly four hours and there was still no sign of her.

"Where is she?" muttered Ryan, saying aloud what they had both been thinking. "She should be back by now. There's a reasonable wind, so it can't have taken much more than an hour to get back home. And then she should be able to bring help quickly in a motor-boat."

Kendra said nothing but she had been thinking exactly the same thing. They continued to gaze out to sea, waiting for a boat to appear. Once or twice a boat seemed to be coming their way but then it turned and went off in another direction.

Slowly the sun slipped beneath the trees and disappeared, leaving a pinky glow on the distant mountains. Ryan and Kendra decided they would sleep near the shaft opening in order to keep Nathan company. They carried their sleeping bags and mattresses from the camp and laid them out on the ground. They brought Nathan's sleeping bag as well and, rolling it into a tight ball, sent it down the shaft.

Nathan couldn't see the sun setting but he could tell it was getting dark. Soon he could barely make out the figures of Ryan and Kendra at the mouth of the shaft. He felt quite miserable as he realized he would have to spend the night alone in the tunnel. Although it wasn't particularly late, he was exhausted from the day's events. So he rolled out his sleeping bag on the tunnel floor and crawled in, soon falling into a fitful sleep.

Ryan and Kendra lay in their sleeping bags talking softly. They were now more concerned about what had become of Claire than about Nathan. What could have happened? The weather had been fine and she should have had no problem getting help and being back well before sunset. They could only assume something had gone wrong, but what?

"I guess we'll have to wait until morning now to find out," said Ryan. "Why don't you go to sleep? We can take shifts staying awake."

Kendra agreed and rolled over, pulling her sleeping bag around her. Soon he could hear her breathing deeply beside him. Ryan lay back and gazed up at the stars. It was a beautiful night to be sleeping outside he decided. He could see the Big Dipper from where he lay and followed its line to the North Star, which shone brightly. The moon, which was nearly full, was rising behind him and the arbutus trees were lit up like silvery ghosts.

Ryan yawned, feeling sleepy all of a sudden. He wished Kendra was still awake to talk to. He shook his head to stay awake and tried to think about all the things that had happened over the past few days. But his eyes were heavy and he struggled to keep them open. Maybe he could just close his eyes and rest a bit but not actually sleep...

* * *

Meanwhile, back on *Pegasus* Claire was also watching the sun set, with even greater dismay. She was miles from her destination and drifting aimlessly.

With no one on board, *Pegasus* had only sailed a short distance before tipping over. Clutching the broken tiller, Claire swam over and pulled down on the centreboard to tip the boat upright again. She clambered back on board and looked at the broken stub of tiller that remained, trying to turn it without success. Then she pulled it out of the rudder and tried to see if the broken piece would go in its place. But the end was too large to fit.

Claire slumped in the bottom of the boat, wondering what to do. Then she thought for a moment. Windsurfers and kiteboarders manage to steer their boards without a rudder. Perhaps the same thing could be done with *Pegasus*. She released the pins at the stern and pulled the rudder out, placing it in the bottom of the boat. She slowly pulled in the sail until it filled with wind. Immediately *Pegasus* swung around and started off downwind. Claire struggled to hang on, letting the sail in and out to change direction and leaning over the side to keep it balanced. She found she could more or less keep *Pegasus* on a wobbly course toward the shore. But the direction she was now going was taking her much further north, to an area with few houses and even fewer beaches to land on. And the effort of constantly pulling on the sail was making her arms very tired.

It was slow going with the boat swinging back and forth rather than taking a nice straight line. As the sun went down Claire found herself getting close to the shore, but there was nowhere to land. The coastline here was high and rocky. She began to feel desperate. Once it was dark it would be impossible to see if it was safe to land. And the effort of keeping *Pegasus* under control had exhausted her.

Finally, just as the light was disappearing she saw a small bay with a cottage above. Heaving a sigh of relief she forced *Pegasus* in that direction and soon felt the bow nudge onto the sandy beach. Claire hopped out and pulled the boat up above the high tide line. She quickly took down the sail and packed it away and then made her way to an old buoy hanging from a tree branch. Buoys or floats hanging on the edge of a beach usually indicated a trail, and sure enough, tucked in the trees was a set of stairs leading up to the cottage. She climbed carefully to the top, feeling her way in the dark. She had given her flashlight to Nathan, not thinking she would need it. At the top there was a little cottage, which was completely dark. She knocked on the door but there was no answer.

Claire didn't want to break into the cottage but she felt this was enough of an emergency to justify doing so. All she needed was a telephone to call for help. She picked up a stone from the ground and went to the porch door, which had a small window in it. If she broke the window she could reach in and unlock the door. She was about to smash the glass when she had a sudden thought. Putting down the rock, she walked around to the back of the house and looked up. Then she circled the entire cottage, groaning inwardly. There were no wires coming into it at any point. No electricity, no telephone.

At the back of the house was a dirt track leading into the forest. Claire sighed. She was cold and wet and hungry and it looked like her only option was to walk for help. And it would probably be a long walk.

* * *

Ryan awoke to a wet nose nuzzling his face. Meg was pawing him and whining softly. He pushed her away and turned over, but then he heard the sound of loud angry voices. He sat up, trying to think where he was. Suddenly he remembered and looked over to the shaft opening where he could see a faint glow of light. The voices were coming from inside the tunnel. He leaned over and shook Kendra awake, covering her mouth with his hand and putting a finger to his lips. He pointed to the opening and the two of them crept over, followed by Meg. They peered in and what they saw made their hearts stop.

On the floor of the tunnel, Nathan cowered in his sleeping bag, a flashlight beam on his face. A voice was angrily barking out questions as he lay there.

"Who are you? How did you get in here? How long

have you been here?"

Nathan nervously tried to explain how he'd fallen down the hole. There were two men pointing their flashlights at him. The first man was big and burly, with a shaved head. He was the one asking the questions and he looked very angry. The second man was short and wiry, with his hair in a ponytail. He didn't say anything but just stood there with a sinister smile on his face. Looking down from above, Kendra nudged Ryan and pointed. It was the man who had tried to swamp their boat on their first day of sailing!

"Who else is with you?" said the burly man to Nathan. "You couldn't have come here alone."

"They went to get help," said Nathan in a shaky voice.

"All of them?"

"Yes, they all went."

"He's lying," said the second man. "They wouldn't have all gone for help. They'd have left somebody here with him." He stepped forward and gave Nathan's sleeping bag a sharp kick.

This was too much for Meg, who was also watching from the top of the shaft. She gave a loud bark and growled angrily.

"Someone's up there!" the first man said. "Go get them!"

The second man started running toward the tunnel entrance.

"Look out! He's coming to get you!" yelled Nathan.

Ryan and Kendra needed no further encouragement. They ran from the shaft opening toward the forest with Meg at their heels. It was very dark and difficult to see. Kendra had put on her sandals when she got up, but Ryan was in bare feet. Just before reaching the trees he felt a sharp pain in his left foot as he stepped on a jagged piece of rock. He hobbled along behind Kendra, grimacing and trying not to put any weight on his left leg.

Ahead of them the light from a flashlight danced on the trees. It was joined by a second, much brighter beam, coming from the little cove. The men must have radioed the boat and are using a searchlight, thought Ryan in a panic. When they reached the forest they went in a short way and stopped. Turning around they could see the light behind them in the distance. But it was still a long way off and moving slowly.

"He's probably having almost as tough a time with the terrain in the dark as we are," whispered Ryan. He bent down and touched his throbbing foot and winced. It felt wet with blood. "I've cut my foot!" he said. "I can't go much farther like this, I'm going to have to find a place to hide."

Kendra nodded. "We can hide around here somewhere. I don't think it's likely he will find us in the dark," she said.

"No, you keep going. It's better if we split up, then at least they won't catch both of us. And you can go a lot further with your sandals. I'll stay here with Meg."

Kendra protested but Ryan insisted. Grudgingly she left him and set off deeper into the forest, picking her way in the dark. She could see his point that it would be better to split up, but was nervous to continue on her own in the dark.

Ryan settled down behind a large fallen log and held Meg close to him, his heart pounding. The ship's searchlight had been turned off and the man with the flashlight didn't seem to be getting any closer. After a few minutes, the flashlight beam disappeared as well. Perhaps they've given up, thought Ryan with relief. Now he could just wait until the men left.

Kendra continued deeper into the forest until she came to the trail that led from the camp to the cove. There she stopped, wondering what to do next. Although she knew it was probably best to just find a place in the woods to hide, she didn't like the idea of staying on her own in the murky darkness. Instead she decided to follow the path to the cove to see if she could see anything. She was sure to notice the men's flashlights if they came up the path and could duck into the woods again.

She crept slowly along the path, keeping alert for

any noises or lights until she emerged at the mossy slope above the cove. Below her the beach was lit by the moonlight and the men's dinghy was pulled up on the sand. She heard footsteps as the two men emerged from the bushes. To her surprise, they were carrying out a number of the paintings, which they put in the dinghy before returning to the tunnel.

Of course! she thought. Now that we've discovered their hiding place they'll need to move the art somewhere else! Sure enough, the men came back with more paintings and put them in the dinghy. It was fairly full now and only one man went back to the tunnel, while the other pushed the dinghy into the water.

They must be leaving, thought Kendra. Good, maybe they'll let Nathan go now. She watched as the man with the ponytail waited by the dinghy. She saw him pull a small radio out of his pocket and say something into it. A crackling reply came back. The man looked expectantly toward the tunnel entrance. A few moments later the second man came back out, pushing Nathan in front of him.

To Kendra's horror, instead of letting him go, the man marched him down to the beach. He pushed Nathan roughly into the little dinghy and rowed out to the fishing boat, taking him with them!

He pushed Nathan roughly into the dinghy.

~ 18 ~

A Bold Move

Nathan was very scared. He was sitting in the hold of the fishing boat, hugging his knees and wondering what was going to happen to him.

After Meg had barked and the man with the ponytail ran out, the burly man had pulled out a handheld radio and called the fishing boat, explaining what had happened. There was a string of curses on the other end of the radio and then a pause. The man waited expectantly until the radio crackled again.

"Bring all the stuff to the beach and load it in the dinghy! We'll have to take everything and find another hiding place!"

"What about these kids?"

"Bring the one you've got back to the boat. The boss can decide what to do with him. And forget about the others, we'll never find them in the dark!"

The man grunted in agreement and put the radio back in his pocket. Ignoring Nathan, he began carrying the paintings out to the cove. Nathan thought about trying to escape, but just as he was about to get up, the ponytail man came back.

"Sit down!" he snarled. "Don't move until I say so or it will be the worse for you!" He went back down the tunnel to assist his accomplice. Nathan could hear their footsteps coming and going as they emptied the tunnel of its treasure. It didn't take long before the man came back.

"Get up!" he ordered. When Nathan didn't move he grabbed him roughly by the arm and pushed him ahead. Nathan stumbled along the tunnel trying not to trip on the rough rock surface. He was shaking but tried to hide the fear he was feeling. Together they went down the beach to the dinghy where the burly man was waiting.

"Get in," he said, pointing to a space in the front. Nathan did as he was told. As he sat down he looked back at the island, trying to see if he could spot Kendra or Ryan. But it was too dark to see anything. At least they weren't captured, he thought thankfully.

They rowed out to where the fishing boat was anchored. A rope ladder was thrown over the side and the dinghy pulled up to it. Grabbing hold of the ladder with one hand, the large man indicated with a nod of his head that Nathan was to climb up. He climbed slowly, not wanting to slip in the dark. At the top of the ladder, a pair of hands grabbed his arms and pulled him on board. There were two other men standing on the deck but he couldn't make out their faces in the dark. Nobody spoke as he was led to the front of the boat by one of the men. A hatch was opened and he was pushed inside, the hatch door closing behind him. He heard a bolt slide closed, locking him in.

Nathan felt his way around the locker. It was empty except for some raingear and a couple of blankets. The steel floor of the hatch was cold and hard so he arranged the blankets to sit on. After a while, he pulled on one of the raincoats to stay warm. Then he sat in the dark and waited.

* * *

Kendra watched them take Nathan to the boat and out of sight below decks. The men unloaded the paintings onto the ship and the dinghy rowed back to the cove. There was a large stack of paintings remaining on shore and she thought it would take at least two more trips to transfer them all to the bigger boat.

She looked at her watch; it was a quarter past three. The sun wouldn't rise for another couple of hours and she couldn't expect help to arrive before dawn. By then the men and their stolen loot would be gone, taking Nathan with them. She wanted to stop them, but how? She wished Ryan was with her, he would know what to do.

She considered swimming out to the boat to try and rescue Nathan. But there was no way of getting on board since the men had pulled the rope ladder back up. And she didn't want to be caught herself, which would just make things worse.

Suddenly she had an idea. What if she could somehow prevent the boat from leaving? Perhaps by tangling something in the propellers? She thought of the old fishing net in the cove that had been washed up by the tide. If it could be wrapped around the propellers it just might jam them!

She glanced down into the cove, where the men were pushing the dinghy back into the water with their second load of boxes. Kendra crept down the rocks to the beach as they began to row. She crossed to the other side where the fishing net was, keeping low to the ground so as not to be seen. She picked up the net, which was thick and heavy and covered in seaweed. It took all her strength to lug it to the water's edge. But once in the water, the net began to float and felt much lighter. She looked to see where the dinghy was; it was just approaching the fishing boat.

Kendra began to swim to the mouth of the cove, using one arm to paddle while the other held the net. The water felt surprisingly warm after being out in the cool night air. She tried not to make any splashes with her hands or feet, but it was difficult to avoid if she was to make any progress with the net dragging behind her. She kept glancing at the fishing boat where they were now unloading the boxes. She reached the mouth of the cove as the dinghy started back. As the dinghy came close she stopped swimming and submerged herself as much as possible, with only her eyes and nose sticking out. She held her breath, hoping the men wouldn't spot her. But they were intent on their job and rowed past without even glancing in her direction.

She watched them go back into the cove and continued on her way. As she approached the stern of the fishing boat she slowed down and again tried to splash as little as possible. Reaching the boat she put her hand out and touched the hull. It was covered in seaweed and barnacles below the waterline and she recoiled slightly at the slimy touch. Looking down the water seemed impenetrable and Kendra wondered how she would be able to see what she was doing. Well, she thought, she was here now and she'd just have to try.

Taking a deep breath, she dove down, pulling the net behind her. Luckily the propellers were a shiny silver and in spite of the gloom she could just make them out against the black hull. There were two propellers, one on each side about a metre apart. She tried to pull the net over the nearest propeller but the holes were too small. Carefully feeling around with her fingers she found a spot where the net was torn. Looping that over one blade of the propeller, she twisted the net around the other blades. By now Kendra was out of breath and shot back to the surface. Although she tried to be quiet, she couldn't control herself as she broke through the surface with a loud splash, gasping for air.

"What was that?" a voice growled from the deck above. A bright flashlight shone down on the water, inches from her face!

Saved by a Seal

Kendra froze and sunk down low in the water as the light came toward her. Suddenly there was a splash a few metres away and a soft *Arf Arf* came across the water.

"It's just a seal," said a voice and the light went out.

Kendra drew deep breaths, trying to stop herself from shaking. The dinghy was now returning from the cove, loaded up with more boxes. She needed to finish putting the net on before they got back. She took another deep breath and dove down to the net. She grabbed the end and swam to the other propeller. She wrapped the net around it and tied it in a big knot. Then she swam back to the surface. No one paid any attention to her splashes this time. The dinghy was approaching the boat and Kendra swam carefully away, heading for the shore.

As she pulled herself out of the water onto the rocks, there was a splash just behind her. She turned and could just make out the shape of a seal in the water nearby.

"Thank you," Kendra whispered softly to the seal. "You saved me out there!"

The seal gave another gentle *Arf Arf* as if to say

'You're welcome!' and sunk under the water.

* * *

Kendra made her way across the rocks into the cove. She collected her shoes from the beach and went back up the path toward the campsite. She was cold and wet and needed some dry clothes, but didn't have the energy. So she sat down on a patch of soft moss and tried to catch her breath.

Suddenly she felt a hand on her shoulder and jumped, her heart beating wildly.

"It's only me," said Ryan in a whisper. Kendra was so relieved she flung her arms around him and squeezed him tightly. Meg jumped at her excitedly, trying to lick her face.

"You're soaking wet!" said Ryan. "What have you been doing?"

Kendra told him how she had seen them take Nathan on board and then swum out with the fishing net to jam the propellers. Ryan listened in amazement.

"Are you crazy?" he exclaimed. "You could have been captured! Or killed! What if the engines had turned on while you were down there?"

Kendra shrugged. "I didn't think it was very likely while they were still loading the boxes."

They both looked over at the fishing boat, where the men had finished loading their cargo and were pulling the dinghy up over the stern. The engines started and there was a rattle as the anchor chain was raised. Kendra and Ryan glanced at each other nervously.

* * *

From his place in the hatch, Nathan heard the engines turn on, causing the ship to vibrate gently. He heard the motors being shifted into gear, followed by a grinding noise and a high pitched whine. There was some loud yelling up above and the engines went quiet again. A moment later the grinding began again, with more shouts. The engine ran a little longer this time before going back to the low rumble, and finally turning off completely. He heard footsteps running above him and a shout saying something about the propellers. This was followed by a great deal of cursing and the anchor was let out again.

The four men congregated on the deck of the ship and an animated argument ensued. "Well, go down there and untangle it!" ordered the burly man who had been in the tunnel with Nathan. The man with the ponytail got out the rope ladder and, after clipping it to two hooks on the railing, threw it over the side. The dinghy was lowered and two men climbed down into it and rowed to the back of the boat. One of them used a pole with a hook on the end to prod at the propellers, trying to unhook the net. But running the engines had caused the net to get much more entangled than Kendra had initially left it, and no amount of prodding or pulling would unhook it.

In the east, the sky was just beginning to brighten. The men's actions became more feverish. They were no longer making any effort to keep quiet and were loudly cursing and arguing. Finally, one of them peeled off his shirt and shoes and jumped into the water with a waterproof flashlight in his hand. He dove down to the propellers and came up again shortly.

"It's hopeless," he yelled up to the deck. "Both propellers are completely tangled in fishing net! We'll need a diver to get them free."

There was another burst of cursing from the deck and one of the men threw his hat down and stomped on it. Finally, a decision must have been made, because they stopped arguing and the two men on deck went below. They emerged with a couple of duffle bags, which they slung over the side to the men waiting below in the dinghy. Then they climbed down the ladder. One of them picked up the oars and began rowing, and they slowly set off toward the far shore.

Back on the bluff Kendra and Ryan looked at each other in astonishment. "They're leaving!" exclaimed Ryan.

"It will take them a long time to row all that way," said Kendra. They looked out at the little dinghy, which was getting smaller and smaller as it moved away from the island. Suddenly they looked at each other.

"Nathan!" they both shouted at the same time. Running down to the beach, they pulled off their socks and shoes, jumped into the water, and swam toward the fishing boat. Kendra reached it first and pulled herself up the ladder, which had been left hanging over the side. Ryan was not far behind her.

On board the boat, they called out Nathan's name. Immediately there was a muffled reply, followed by a loud banging. They rushed into the cabin of the fishing boat and followed the banging to the front. Ryan unlocked the door of the hatch and Nathan almost fell out on top of them.

"What happened? Where are the men?" he asked, looking around wildly as if they might return at any moment.

"They've gone," said Ryan. "Kendra jammed the propellers so the boat wouldn't start, and now they're trying to row across to the other shore."

Nathan looked at Kendra admiringly. "So that's what happened," he said. "I knew there was something wrong with the engines, but I couldn't tell what it was. Did they take the stolen loot with them?"

"No," said Ryan. "The dinghy is pretty full with the four of them in it and I think they wanted to get away as quickly as possible."

"Well that's good," said Nathan. "But it's too bad they're getting away. Nothing we can do about it though."

"Maybe there is!" said Ryan. "There must be a radio on this boat. We could try calling for help." They went back to the wheelhouse and looked around. Sure enough, there was a VHF radio mounted next to the wheel.

Ryan picked up the mouthpiece and pushed the talk button. "Hello, anybody out there?"

Kendra giggled. "Aren't you supposed to say something like 'Mayday' or 'Emergency'?"

Ryan pushed the talk button again. "Emergency! Emergency! Calling all boats, please respond!"

There was a pause and the radio crackled in response. "This is Maple Harbour Marine Search and Rescue. Please identify yourselves and state the nature of your emergency."

"This is Ryan Seto. We're on a boat at Whalebone Island and my cousin was kidnapped by a gang of thieves. He's free but the thieves are getting away!"

The voice on the radio began to say something but was suddenly interrupted by a shriek. Claire's voice came over the radio. "Ryan, where are you? What's happened? Where's Nathan?"

Quickly Ryan explained what had happened, keeping it as brief as possible. "But the men are trying to escape in the dinghy now! We need to stop them!" he finished.

"We're on our way," said Claire. "We should be there in a few minutes. Hang on!"

Ryan hung up the mouthpiece and all three went back up on the deck of the fishing boat. The sun was now up and the sight of it made them realize how cold they were. Nathan went back down below to bring some blankets from the hatch where he had been locked up.

Off in the distance, they could still see the dinghy, although by now it was just a speck. The men had made it about halfway to the shore.

"I wish they would hurry up," said Kendra. As she spoke there was a faint noise in the distance. It grew louder as a red and yellow motor boat came around the corner at full speed, waves foaming at its bow.

"It's the Search and Rescue boat!" cried Ryan.

"And the police!" added Kendra as another boat, this one dark blue with the words POLICE clearly marked on its hull, came into view.

All three children began to wave frantically. The two boats roared toward them and then slowed as they drew near. In addition to the crew, Claire, Uncle William, and Aunt Jennie were on board the Search and Rescue boat. On the police boat, Sergeant Sandhu poked his head out of the cockpit and waved. Two other police officers were with him.

"Over there!" Ryan shouted, pointing at the dinghy in the distance. "They're getting away!"

Sergeant Sandhu looked in the direction he was pointing and then disappeared back into the cockpit. The engines on the police boat roared to life again and it shot off in the direction of the dinghy.

By this time the Search and Rescue boat had pulled up beside the fishing boat and Aunt Jennie was coming up the rope ladder with Claire and Uncle William right behind her. She picked Nathan up and gave him a big hug, while Claire and Uncle William did the same to Ryan and Kendra. Aunt Jennie put Nathan down and stepped back to look at him.

"You don't look too bad for having fallen down a mineshaft and been kidnapped," she said with smile. Nathan shrugged and nodded. Then he looked at his mother quizzically.

"Did you bring any food?" he asked. "I'm starving!"

~ 20 ~

The Real Treasure

Nathan followed Aunt Jennie and Uncle William down the ladder to the Search and Rescue boat with Claire, Kendra, and Ryan close behind. Sure enough, Aunt Jennie had thought to bring some muffins along and they dug into them hungrily. By this time the police had apprehended the thieves. Before setting off for Maple Harbour, the police boat returned to Whalebone Island to drop off Sergeant Sandhu. The children went back to the island with Aunt Jennie, Uncle William, and the police officer to collect their things. First they went to check out the mine tunnel where the thieves had stored their loot. Sergeant Sandhu had retrieved the key to the door from the man with the ponytail, so they were able to enter the tunnel the proper way for the first time. Nathan showed them where he had fallen through the shaft.

"Yikes! You're lucky you weren't seriously hurt," said Sergeant Sandhu, shaking his head.

With everyone there to help it took no time at all to dismantle the camp and bring it down to the cove, where it was packed into the waiting Search and Rescue boat.

"Gee, we almost forgot," said Claire as they were

stowing the last of the gear. She reached into one of the bags and pulled out the items they had found on the sunken boat. "With everything else going on we forget to tell you we found the sunken wreck!" Sergeant Sandhu peered at the objects with interest.

"You're sure it was the *Gypsy Moth*?" said Aunt Jennie.

"Yes, we could see the name on the stern," said Ryan.

Sergeant Sandhu picked up the pink bunny by one ear and looked at it. "We'll return these things to the owner. I don't know if he'll actually want this stuff back, but I'm sure he'll be interested to hear about his boat."

* * *

Back home the four children claimed to not be tired at all. But it wasn't long before the first yawns appeared and Aunt Jennie insisted they get some sleep. It was well into the afternoon before they emerged from their rooms again.

Now they were gathered on the outdoor patio to enjoy a barbecued salmon dinner. Uncle William had been fishing with a friend while the children were camping on the island and had caught a big sockeye salmon. He cooked it on the barbecue to celebrate everyone's safe arrival back home. In addition to the salmon, there were roasted potatoes and corn on the cob. And for dessert, a blackberry pie with vanilla ice cream.

"Mmm, I'm starving," said Nathan as he piled potatoes high on his plate. "I missed breakfast and lunch today." Everyone was very hungry and they dug into their food enthusiastically. While they ate, Claire filled them in on her adventures with the broken tiller and why it had taken so long for her to get home.

"So where is *Pegasus* now?" asked Kendra.

"I don't know exactly," replied Claire. "Somewhere along the coast. She's safe enough for now, but I'd like to get her back as soon as possible. Although I can't sail back with a broken tiller," she added gloomily. "There goes all my savings; a new tiller is expensive."

"Well," her dad said. "*Pegasus* might be closer than you think." Claire looked at him, her eyebrows raised. "Search and Rescue went and found her and towed her back. She's down on the dock."

Claire jumped to her feet and ran to the edge of the garden. There by the dock was her boat, just as her father had said. She came back to the table with a big smile on her face.

"That was nice of them," she said. "I'll have to give them a big thank you."

As she sat down a car door slammed and a moment later Sergeant Sandhu came around the side of the house.

"Hope I'm not disturbing you," he said. He was carrying an envelope in his hand.

"Not at all, Raj," said Aunt Jennie. "You're just in time for pie."

"Don't mind if I do," he said with a smile, pulling up a chair.

He turned to the children. "I've spent the day going through all the art pieces. Unfortunately, several are missing. They must be the ones which were taken to be sold the first night you saw them come to the island. The men we captured are refusing to talk, so I wasn't too optimistic that we'd be able to find those pieces or the ringleaders." He paused for a moment.

"Except for a funny coincidence," he went on. "First thing this morning I returned the items from the *Gypsy Moth* to their owner. He was very interested to finally know what had happened to his boat. His daughter was also pleased to get her rabbit back. But he told me that the cell phone didn't belong to him. So I figured it must have belonged to the thief. The phone doesn't work of course, but we were able to take the memory card out of it." Everyone watched him expectantly.

"Turns out that phone belonged to one of the men we caught today, the one with the ponytail. And on that memory card, we found a full list of all his contacts, including an export company we've been suspicious about for a while. The police just raided a warehouse in the city belonging to that company this afternoon and we found the missing paintings as well as other stolen art from all over the country.

"So you might not have found any treasure on the *Gypsy Moth*, but that cell phone turned out to be a treasure trove for us! It's allowed us to break up one of the biggest art theft rings in the country!"

Everyone looked at him in amazement. Sergeant Sandhu sat back in his chair, pleased at the reaction his story had received.

"Wow, we were a bit disappointed with what we found on the wreck," said Claire. "What luck that the two cases turned out to be linked!"

Sergeant Sandhu filled them in on some more details while Aunt Jennie served the blackberry pie. When he was done he thanked them and got up to leave.

"Oh, one more thing," he said, turning around. "I heard *Pegasus* has a broken tiller. I'm afraid there's no official reward for recovering the art, but a few of us down at the detachment thought you deserved something for your efforts." He held out an envelope to Claire, who opened it and pulled out a gift certificate to the local marine store.

"It's not a lot," he said. "But it should be enough

for a new tiller."

Everyone gave a cheer. Claire thanked him and looked very pleased.

After Sergeant Sandhu had left, Aunt Jennie dished out second helpings of pie. They sat and ate their pie and watched the setting sun.

"I can't believe we have to leave tomorrow," said Ryan, and Kendra nodded glumly in agreement. Things had been so busy that they had hardly thought about their parents. Now they realized how much they missed them. But they also didn't want the summer to end and felt sad about leaving.

"You can always come back next year," said Aunt Jennie, giving his arm a squeeze. "I'm just glad we didn't have to tell your parents we'd lost you!" Everyone laughed, and Ryan nodded and bit his lip. He helped clear the table and then stood on the patio looking out at the sea. The sun was low in the sky and bathed everything in a warm glow. In the distance, a tug was towing a boom of logs down the strait, while in front of him he could see *Pegasus* bobbing gently. It's been the best summer holiday ever, he thought.

Suddenly he saw a strange puff of spray in the water just outside the bay. He stared for a moment and then he saw it again.

"Hey, what's that?" he cried. The others jumped up and looked to where he was pointing. Another puff of spray appeared.

"It's the whale!" cried Kendra.

Claire rushed to the house to grab the binoculars. The humpback whale came closer and they could see its back breaking the surface of the water. Taking turns with the binoculars, they watched as it swam back and forth in front of them. It moved gracefully through the water, in spite of its huge size. A few times it breached, coming almost completely out of the water and landing with a splash. Finally, it began to swim away toward the point.

Ryan watched it go, then he put out his hand and gave it a little wave. "Goodbye," he said softly. "See you next year!"

The End

About the Author

Michael Wilson lives in Gibsons, British Columbia with his family and dog, Meg. When not writing, he likes to sail his Flying Junior in the waters of Howe Sound. *Adventure on Whalebone Island* is his first book for children.

* * *

Did you enjoy reading *Adventure on Whalebone Island?* We'd love to hear from you! Look for more adventures with Claire, Ryan, Kendra, Nathan, and Meg, coming soon!

Rainy Bay Press
PO Box 1911
Gibsons, BC
V0N 1V0

www.rainybaypress.ca

Made in the USA
Charleston, SC
09 December 2016